THE HUNTERS AND THE HUNTED

Slocum was riding the Appaloosa, Delaney the roan. They had just started up the slope when a red ray from the lowering sun glinted garishly off something at the top of the hill.

Slocum pitched out of the saddle without thinking, and while he was in midair he heard the flat *whap!* of a heavy-caliber bullet passing through the space he had just occupied. The dull boom of the rifle came an instant later, as Slocum was slamming into the ground and rolling over. . . . Another slug whipped by as Slocum scrambled to his feet and lunged toward the Appaloosa. An ugly thud sounded, and the horse let out a shrill whinny of pain.

Slocum sprawled behind the dead horse, using it for cover as he lined his Winchester on the top of the hill and started firing. . . .

DON'T MISS THESE
ALL-ACTION WESTERN SERIES
FROM THE BERKLEY PUBLISHING GROUP

THE GUNSMITH by J. R. Roberts
Clint Adams was a legend among lawmen, outlaws, and ladies.
They called him . . . the Gunsmith.

LONGARM by Tabor Evans
The popular long-running series about U.S. Deputy Marshal
Long—his life, his loves, his fight for justice.

SLOCUM by Jake Logan
Today's longest-running action Western. John Slocum rides a
deadly trail of hot blood and cold steel.

BUSHWHACKERS by B. J. Lanagan
An action-packed series by the creators of Longarm! The rousing
adventures of the most brutal gang of cutthroats ever assembled—
Quantrill's Raiders.

JAKE LOGAN

SLOCUM AND THE TEXAS ROSE

J

JOVE BOOKS, NEW YORK

SLOCUM AND THE TEXAS ROSE

A Jove Book / published by arrangement with
the author

PRINTING HISTORY
Jove edition / April 1998

The Penguin Putnam Inc. World Wide Web site address is
http://www.penguinputnam.com

ISBN: 0-515-12264-5

A JOVE BOOK®
Jove Books are published by The Berkley Publishing Group, a member
of Penguin Putnam Inc.,
200 Madison Avenue, New York, New York 10016.
JOVE and the "J" design are trademarks
belonging to Jove Publications, Inc.

PRINTED IN THE UNITED STATES OF AMERICA

10 9 8 7 6 5 4 3 2 1

1

The blue norther hit at midday. Slocum found the woman an hour later.

He had been riding across the high plains of the Texas Panhandle for what seemed like weeks now, even though he knew it hadn't really been that long. He had cut down through the Sangre de Cristos from Colorado, through the corner of New Mexico at Raton Pass, and then ridden on into Texas before turning south toward Tascosa. A posse had chased him out of Pueblo after the local law had recognized him from an old reward dodger, but he had long since shaken them off his trail. He figured he'd stop in Tascosa. It would feel good to rest for a few days and maybe find a woman to pamper him before he moved on. In the back of his mind, he was thinking about wintering in San Antonio. It stayed warm there most of the time, the *señoritas* were pretty, and he could always find a poker game in the Buckhorn Saloon. It sounded like a good plan to Slocum.

But he might not even make Tascosa before winter set in. All morning he had been glancing back over his shoulder to the north, watching the thin line of dark blue clouds on the horizon that had marched steadily closer. Just before noon the breeze that had been blowing gently in his face from the south abruptly died down, and the air went still. Slocum knew what

1

that meant. He reined the rangy lineback dun to a stop and hipped around in the saddle to dig out his sheepskin coat from the saddlebags. No sooner had he put the coat on than the north wind hit.

It was hard, raw, and cold. Slocum was reminded of the old saying about how there was nothing between Tascosa and the north pole except a picket fence. Sure as hell felt like it right now, he thought as he put his back to the wind, pulled his Stetson down tight on his head, and hunched his shoulders deeper into the coat. The dun let out a whicker of complaint, and Slocum said, "Could be worse, hoss. At least we're not heading into the wind."

This wasn't the first time in his life he'd been cold. Nor would it be the last, he told himself. He kept riding, hoping that he would reach Tascosa by nightfall. As fast as the temperature was plummeting, if he was caught out on the plains after dark with no shelter, he'd likely freeze to death.

There was an area of rough gullies up ahead, he remembered from a previous trip through this region. If worst came to worst, maybe he could hole up in one of them and find enough dry brush to build a fire. At least that way he would be out of the howling wind.

With that wind behind him, he didn't hear the angry shouts and the terrified screams until he was almost right on top of the trouble. He reined in as the first faint noises drifted to his ears. The ground was already starting to fall away in a series of arroyos. The ruckus was coming from the one right in front of him, but it was off to the side a ways. Slocum considered for a second. Whatever was happening, it was none of his business. The banks of the gully weren't steep. He could ride down this side, across the flat bed of the arroyo, and up the opposite bank in a matter of moments. Whatever was going on around the bend could run its course without him.

He heeled the dun into motion again and rode down into the gully. Movement to the right caught his eye, and even though he knew it was a stupid thing to do, he looked.

Around the nearest twisting turn of the arroyo came a

woman, running desperately, skirts flapping and the scarf around her throat whipping behind her. Slocum saw a young, pretty face and a lot of curly blond hair.

About ten feet behind the woman were three men in hot pursuit. They couldn't run very fast because of the long, bulky buffalo-hide coats they wore, but their legs were longer than the woman's and they were steadily cutting the gap between them and her.

"Shit!"

The heartfelt curse hissed out between Slocum's gritted teeth. He should have moved a little faster, should have put this arroyo behind him sooner so that he wouldn't have seen what was going on. Now, the sight of the frightened woman told him that he was going to have to take a hand in this game, whatever it was.

He reined the dun around so that he was facing the woman and her pursuers. They were only about twenty feet from him now, and none of them seemed to have noticed him yet. The woman finally did, though, and she stumbled in surprise at the sight of him. That slowed her down enough so that one of the men chasing her decided to launch himself at her in a running tackle. His arms went around her and bore her to the rocky ground on the floor of the gully. The breath went out of her in a pained *whoosh* as his weight landed on top of her.

Slocum's hand reached smoothly into the open front of his coat and closed around the butt of the Colt Navy holstered in a cross-draw rig on his left hip. He palmed it out with practiced ease and lined the barrel in the general direction of the three men as he eared back the hammer.

"That's enough, gents," he called out, raising his voice so that he could be heard over the wind.

The man lying on top of the woman planted an elbow in her back, bringing a cry of pain from her as she was pressed against the rough ground. He looked up at Slocum, forced to crane his neck quite a bit to do so since he was prone and Slocum was on horseback. "Who the hell are you?" he demanded.

"The man who's going to kill you if you don't get off that woman," Slocum said bluntly.

"This ain't none o' your business, mister," said one of the other men. "This gal stole from us, and now she's got to pay."

The first man levered himself halfway off the woman and reached down to roughly grasp her rump. "An' she's got the right price too, lemme tell you."

"Come on, mister," said the third man. "Put that gun away and we'll let you have her after we're through with her. Course, she'll be a mite used by then."

"Help me!" the woman cried piercingly. "For God's sake, mister, help me!"

The man on top of her cuffed her on the side of the head. "Hush up!" he told her. "You stole, and you got to pay."

"What did she steal?" Slocum asked.

"Four biscuits!" the second man said indignantly. "We offered to share our grub with her, an' she repays by hidin' biscuits under her coat."

Slocum didn't lower the Colt. With his other hand, he reached inside the pocket of his jeans and brought out a five-dollar gold piece, the next to the last one he had. He tossed it contemptuously onto the ground near the three men and the woman. "There. That ought to pay for the biscuits. Now leave the woman and get the hell out of here."

The first man shook his head as he continued to crudely fondle the woman trapped underneath him. "No, sir," he declared. "It's a matter of principle now."

It was a matter of rape, that was what it was, Slocum thought. These men—buffalo hunters, from the shaggy, bearded look of them—were determined to have the woman. The stolen biscuits were just a flimsy excuse for them to take what they really wanted.

"Where you boys from?" asked Slocum, taking the men by surprise with the pleasant tone of the question.

One of them jerked a thumb over his shoulder and said, "We got a camp back up the gully a ways."

"Hunting buffalo, are you?"

"That's right. Most of the crews have gone back to Dodge for the winter, so we got the field mostly to ourselves."

Slocum nodded. The almost unimaginably large herds of buffalo that had thronged the Great Plains only a few years earlier had been thinned out considerably, and many of the herds had migrated south from Kansas to the Texas Panhandle. The buffalo hunters, though still operating out of Dodge City, did most of their bloody work in these parts now, and Slocum figured that within another year or two, there would be so few buffalo left that it wouldn't be profitable to hunt them anymore. That was a damned shame, but there was nothing he could do about it. In the meantime, he was faced with these three men who probably weren't even aware that they were nearly relics.

Hell, thought Slocum, he was getting pretty close to being a relic himself. One day soon, this whole part of the country was liable to be civilized.

But not yet. Right now, the Panhandle was still ruled by gun and knife and fist, and Slocum was glad the three hunters didn't have their heavy Sharps buffalo rifles with them. One of those Big Fifties could put a hell of a big hole in a man.

All three of the hunters had shell belts and holstered pistols under their coats, however, which made them plenty dangerous. Slocum considered his options. He couldn't shoot at the first hunter as long as the man was lying on top of the woman; the risk of hitting her instead was too great. He felt confident he could down both of the other men before they even got a shot off, but by that time the man on the ground would be able to draw and shoot Slocum out of the saddle. The smart thing to do would be to back the dun away from them and ride on out of the arroyo. He didn't know the woman, didn't owe her a damned thing.

Instead, he broke into a grin, let down the hammer of the Colt, and slid it back into its holster. The buffalo hunters looked surprised but relieved. They had to have figured that at least one of them might die here today in this desolate arroyo.

"I've done some buffalo hunting myself," said Slocum. "Can you use another man? I don't even mind doing the skinning."

Skinning was the messiest, most disgusting job of all, and if these men didn't already have someone to handle it for them, they might jump at the chance to recruit some help.

But they weren't ready to embrace Slocum like a long-lost brother. The one on the ground peered up at him suspiciously and asked, "What about the woman?"

"She's nothing to me," Slocum said with a shake of his head. "Sorry I got a mite impulsive and nearly mixed into something that doesn't concern me. It ain't worth dying over."

"Now you're gettin' smart, mister," said one of the other men.

"If you don't mind, though," Slocum said as he started to swing down out of the saddle, "I'll just get that gold piece back." He stepped toward the coin.

From the corner of his eye, he saw tears running down the face of the woman as silent sobs shook her. She had counted on him for help, and now it looked as if she wasn't going to get it. He was going to abandon her to the buffalo hunters, perhaps even join in as they violated her.

The man who had tackled her pushed himself to his feet and reached down to tangle his fingers in her hair. "Come on, gal," he said as he started to jerk her up.

Slocum bent over to retrieve the gold piece from the ground with his left hand. As he straightened, he drew the Colt again, aiming and cocking in one efficient motion. The gun bucked in his hand as it roared. The eyes of the hunter who was trying to lift the woman from the ground widened in surprise as the heavy slug struck him in the forehead, bored right on through his brain, and burst out the back of his head in a grisly shower of blood, gray matter, and splintered bone.

Slocum was pivoting and recocking even as the first man died. The other two yelled curses and grabbed for their guns, but they were too slow by half. Slocum's gun boomed again, then again and yet a fourth time. The buffalo hunters were driven backward by the bullets thudding into their chests. One of them sprawled motionless on the ground. The other man twitched a time or two before he lay still.

The shots echoed back from the walls of the gully, gradually fading away.

Slocum remembered to breathe. He drew a deep lungful of air into his body, blew it out in a gusty sigh. The temperature had dropped enough so that his breath fogged in the air. The sky overhead was a dull, leaden gray by now, and Slocum felt faint touches of moisture on his cheeks that he knew were the first grains of blowing snow.

Holding the Colt ready, he went to each body in turn and prodded it with his boot until he was sure the buffalo hunters were all dead. Wasn't much doubt about the first one, he thought. Most of that man's brains had leaked out the hole in the back of his head by now. Slocum reloaded and holstered the revolver, then went over to the woman, who was still lying on the ground, shivering. She had put her arms over her head when the shooting started, and there were a few drops of blood from the dead man on the sleeves of her dress.

Slocum bent and took hold of her shoulders. He rolled her over and then caught her under the arms, lifting her with little noticeable effort. She was slender, though suitably curved at breast and hip. Through her tears, she looked up at Slocum with cornflower-blue eyes.

"You . . . you killed them," she said.

"Seemed like the thing to do at the time," Slocum said.

"I . . . thought you were going to . . . to help them rape me."

"They thought that too. Good thing they did." Slocum glanced grimly at the corpses. "Otherwise we might've both been dead before the day was over."

"I . . . I don't know how to thank you. . . ."

Slocum glanced at the sky. The clouds were so thick that he couldn't tell for sure where the sun was. The snow was getting heavier. With this delay, there was no way he could reach Tascosa before the full force of the storm hit.

"Can you find your way back to their camp?" he asked the woman.

"I think so. It . . . it's in this arroyo. You can't really miss it."

Unless the snow started falling so heavily that they might walk right past the camp without seeing it. Blizzards of that force sometimes hit the Panhandle.

"Did they have a tent or any sort of shelter?"

The woman nodded. "Yes, a tent. And a wagon and some mules. They had a fire going. I saw the smoke from it and thought maybe they would help me. . . ." Her voice faded away as she remembered how that hope had turned out.

"Did you really steal their biscuits?" Slocum asked with a bleak chuckle.

"Well, I . . . yes. Yes, I did. But I had a good reason."

"Being hungry's the best reason of all." Slocum took her arm and began leading her toward the dun, which had shied away several yards when the shooting began.

"They weren't for me," the woman said. "I . . . I'm not traveling alone."

Slocum had already been wondering what she was doing out here on the plains. "Was your husband with you?" he asked. "Did something happen to him?"

The woman shook her head. "No. I'm not married." Without explaining, she went on. "Can you take me back to their camp? I have to get back there as soon as I can." Now that she had recovered somewhat from the terror that had gripped her, her voice was a little stronger. She still sounded very worried about something, however.

"That's what I had in mind," Slocum told her. He caught the dun's reins, put a foot in the stirrup, and swung up on the horse's back. Then he leaned over and extended a hand to the woman. "Get up here behind me."

She scrambled aboard the horse, aided by his strong grip. As she put her arms around his waist and hung on, she said, "My name is Rose. Rose Delaney."

"John Slocum," he told her. He heeled the dun into a trot,

heading down the arroyo and leaving the bodies behind him where they had fallen.

"Thank you, Mr. Slocum," Rose said. "You saved my life. You've done more than you know."

Slocum didn't say anything. He was watching the sky through slitted eyes. He'd been through enough blue northers to know that this was going to be a bad one. Snow stung his face, gritty like grains of sand.

If Rose Delaney was truly grateful, she would have ample opportunities to demonstrate it tonight, thought Slocum. They were both going to need all the body heat they could share with each other, just to keep from freezing. Even down here in the arroyo in a tent, out of the worst of the wind, it was going to be colder than a gravedigger's tit, he told himself. No, he thought with a frown, that wasn't the way the old saying went. . . .

"There it is," Rose said.

Slocum saw the tent and the wagon and the picketed mules as he rode around another bend in the gully. He nodded. The north bank was steeper here, and the tent had been pitched right up against it, to cut as much of the wind as possible. The wagon was parked on the west side of the tent, to further block the wind. The mules were picketed to the east. A campfire in front of the tent had burned down to embers that hissed as the tiny flakes of snow struck them.

A horse with a bulky pouch attached to the saddle was tied to the same picket as one of the mules. The woman slid down from the back of the dun even as Slocum was bringing the animal to a halt. She ran across the rock-littered ground to the horse and unfastened the bundle. Then, cradling it against her in her arms, she hurried back to the tent.

Slocum had dismounted and tied the dun to the wagon tongue. He stepped over to the tent and held back the canvas entrance flap for the woman. She ducked inside, still carrying the pouch. Slocum wondered what was inside it. Something mighty valuable to the woman, that was for sure. He was surprised the buffalo hunters hadn't already looted it, whatever it was. But they would have gotten around to it when they finished having their fun with the woman.

Slocum dropped the tent flap and turned back to the dun. He unsaddled quickly and rubbed the sweat dry under the blanket. Then he led the dun over and picketed it with the mules and the other horse. All of them had their rumps turned toward the north as they huddled together for warmth. Slocum hoped they survived the night. He had done all he could for them, which was nothing.

But he could do something for himself. He ducked his head against the stinging snowfall and went to the tent. As he stooped over and stepped through the entrance, he saw that the ground was covered with thick buffalo robes. That was good. He and Rose could roll up in the robes and let nature take its course . . . in more ways than one.

Then he stopped short as he saw what Rose was holding as she sat cross-legged on the robes. She had unwrapped the bundle she'd taken from her horse, and now there was a tiny face looking up at her from a nest of thick blankets. Slocum was damned near struck dumb by the sight.

It was a baby.

2

"It's a baby," Slocum said.

Rose Delaney glanced up at him, smiling faintly. "Of course he is. What else would he be? His name is Edgar."

That was some moniker to stick on a baby, Slocum thought. Then he stopped thinking about the baby's name and asked himself instead what in blue blazes an infant was doing out here in the middle of nowhere.

There was one obvious answer. "He's your son?" Slocum said to Rose.

She shook her head. "No. I wish he was. But I'm just looking after him for a . . . a friend of mine."

Slocum frowned. That didn't make much sense. He didn't know much about motherhood, but it didn't seem likely to him that any woman would entrust her baby to someone who was about to set out across the Panhandle, alone and on horseback.

Slocum moved closer to Rose and hunkered on his heels. He had a naturally curious nature that had gotten him into trouble plenty of times before now, but he wanted to get the straight of this. He said, "That horse tied up out there with the mules is yours, right?"

"That's right," Rose replied with a nod. "I told you, I saw

11

the smoke from the campfire and rode down here into the arroyo looking for help.''

He eyed the dress she wore. It was made of fairly thick material, but the wind from that blue norther would have still cut right through it. ''You're not dressed for traveling in weather like this,'' he commented.

''The weather wasn't like this when I started. It was still rather pleasant, in fact.''

Slocum nodded slowly. ''Texas weather is changeable, all right, especially at this time of year. You might burn up one day and freeze the next.'' He studied her in the dim light that penetrated the tent from outside. Her face was fine-boned, almost delicate, and her skin was fair. She didn't look like the sort of woman to be found anywhere on the frontier, let alone wandering alone across the high plains with a baby.

''You're wondering what I was doing out here,'' Rose said sharply, as if reading his mind. His curiosity had to be plain to see on his rough-hewn face.

''That's your business,'' Slocum said.

''But you made it yours when you risked your life to help me.''

He shrugged. ''You could look at it like that.''

''I'm sorry, Mr. Slocum. I know you saved my life, but there are some things I . . . I just can't tell you.''

''Fair enough,'' Slocum said, though he didn't really think it was fair at all. He gestured at the infant, who was making little gurgling sounds. ''Reckon you must've stolen those biscuits for the baby.''

''Yes, I thought I . . . I could chew them up first and then feed the bites to him, like a mother bird with her babies.''

''Do you have any milk?'' She could take that question one of two ways, he thought, taking it to mean either canned milk or milk from her breasts.

Either way, she shook her head. ''None at all, I'm afraid. I ran out yesterday.''

''Where were you headed?''

''I thought I might go to Santa Fe.''

She was a hell of a long way from Santa Fe, Slocum thought, whether she knew it or not. With this change in the weather, she never would have made it.

"Well, I was on my way to Tascosa," he said. "It's not too far. If the storm blows over tonight without dumping too much snow and ice, we can probably make it into town tomorrow."

"Into Tascosa, you mean?" She sounded as if that idea made her nervous. Slocum saw her eyes darting from side to side for a second, just like those of a trapped animal, before she regained control of herself.

"It's the nearest settlement," he told her. "If you have any money, you can stock up on supplies there, including milk for the little one. Right now, it'd be foolish to try to make it to New Mexico Territory."

She sighed. "You're right, of course, Mr. Slocum."

"Call me John."

"All right . . . John." Another faint smile touched her lips, and Slocum thought she was the most beautiful woman he had seen in a long time. Of course, he hadn't really seen any women since lighting a shuck out of Pueblo.

He started poking around the inside of the tent. In the gear left behind by the dead buffalo hunters he found a candle, and lit it with a lucifer he took from his shirt pocket. The yellow glow of the flame was feeble but welcome. It dispersed some of the shadows inside the tent. By the light of the candle, Slocum rearranged the buffalo robes so that there was a clear spot in the center of the tent. Then he tightened the sheepskin jacket around him and went outside into the gully, returning a few moments later with several good-sized rocks and an armful of dried brush. After arranging the rocks in a circle, he used some of the brush to start a small fire. If he fed the fuel in a little at a time, he could keep the fire going for quite a while. Even a tiny blaze such as the one he built could provide enough heat to make the difference between life and death.

While Slocum was doing that, Rose fed the baby, doing as she had said and softening each bite of biscuit by chewing it first before she placed it in Edgar's mouth. Now that Slocum had gotten a better look at the child, he estimated Edgar's age at about a year. The boy could probably toddle around a little if given the chance, so they would have to keep an eye on him and make sure he didn't get into the fire.

Slocum ventured out into the cold again, fetching a pan from his saddlebags, along with the last of his bacon. He sliced the bacon with his Bowie, and soon the smell of frying meat filled the tent, making his empty belly clench almost painfully. When the bacon was done, Rose took a small piece, crumbled it, and fed that to Edgar as well.

The day before, Slocum had run out of Arbuckle's. He would have given a lot to have a cup of hot coffee right about now, but he didn't brood over its lack. He would just have to replenish his own supplies when he reached Tascosa too.

There was a small smoke hole in the roof of the tent, so the air stayed relatively clear. It grew warmer, though, and Slocum saw Rose's eyelids beginning to droop. It was still afternoon, but with the thick overcast outside, the sky was almost as dark as night, as he saw when he moved the tent flap aside slightly and peered out. He turned back to Rose and said, "You might as well roll up in one of those robes and try to get some sleep. You look tuckered."

"I *am* tired," she admitted. "But someone has to look after Edgar."

The baby was sucking noisily on a piece of cloth Rose had given him. All the sweetness had probably been sucked out of that sugar-tit a long time ago, but Edgar didn't seem to mind. His eyes were closed as he lay in his nest of blankets on the soft pile of robes.

"I'll keep an eye on him," Slocum promised. "Not that he's going to take much watching. He looks pretty tired too."

"This trip has been hard on him," Rose said regretfully.

Slocum still wondered about the details of this puzzling situation, but there would be time enough later to hash them all out, he told himself. Right now, Rose and the baby needed rest.

He moved over alongside Rose and lifted the robe on which she was sitting so that he could wrap it around her shoulders. Settling down next to her, he gently pulled her against him so that she was resting on his hard, muscular frame. Instinctively, she lowered her head onto his chest and made a sound of contentment as she closed her eyes.

Slocum leaned against the side of the gully, the canvas of the tent between him and the earth and stone wall. He pulled one of the robes over him, draping it over Rose as well, and gradually the warmth grew. Slocum meant to stay awake, he truly did.

But it wasn't long before his chin dipped toward his chest and his cheek rested against the top of Rose's head, and he went to sleep with the feel of her in his arms and the fragrance of her hair filling his senses.

Slocum wasn't sure how long he had been asleep. He woke as he usually did, instantly, with all his senses alert.

The wind was still howling out of the northwest above the gully. Cold drafts of it seeped into the tent here and there, but under the buffalo robes, Slocum was comfortably warm. The fire had burned down and gone out, but heat still radiated from the rocks. Rose was snuggled against his side, but she had moved while he was asleep, Slocum saw. The baby, Edgar, was nestled between them.

That made for a mighty domestic-looking scene, Slocum thought wryly. He and Rose might have been husband and wife, with their child resting between them. But Rose wasn't his wife, and if she had been telling the truth, Edgar wasn't even her child. There was something strange going on here, and Slocum resolved to get to the bottom of it—later. When the sun was shining and the air was warm again.

He shifted a little, trying to ease muscles that had grown stiff, and Rose made a small noise in her throat and stirred. Her arm moved, sliding out from the robe wrapped around her, and her hand dropped loosely onto Slocum.

Right onto his groin, as a matter of fact.

He blinked. He felt his manhood stiffening, prodding against the light touch of Rose's palm. His brain knew that she was asleep, that she wasn't trying to arouse him, but the swelling and hardening pole of flesh under her hand had a mind of its own.

She murmured again, and her fingers closed around his shaft and squeezed. Slocum gritted his teeth against a yelp of surprise. Rose caressed him brazenly. Her fingers began to work at the buttons of his trousers.

She had to be awake by now, Slocum thought. No woman could do what she was doing without being aware of it.

But either way, he didn't want her to stop.

She freed his manhood from the tight confines of the denim trousers and gripped the shaft tightly. Slocum groaned. Her hand was so warm and soft that when she started making slow pumping motions, he almost shot off then and there. With a supreme effort of will, he held back.

"Move the baby," Rose whispered, confirming that she was indeed awake.

"You don't have to do this," Slocum told her. Could be she just felt grateful to him for rescuing her from the buffalo hunters, and she wanted to pay him back the only way she could. But if she was going to regret it later, he didn't want her to go ahead.

Of course, from the practiced way she was stroking him, it wasn't very likely that he was dealing with a blushing virgin either. Rose knew what she was doing.

"I want to, John," she whispered. She lifted her head so that she could look up at him. The interior of the tent was too dim for either of them to see the other clearly, but Slocum could feel her gaze on him. She was intent, and she knew what she wanted.

"All right," he said as he reached down and gently picked up the baby. He set Edgar to the side, being careful not to jar the sleeping infant. Edgar made little sucking sounds with his mouth.

Rose pulled up her dress and her petticoat, then lifted her

leg and slid it across Slocum's body. She shifted so that her weight was on him. He reached down between them and found slick, heated flesh, eager for his touch. She let out a gasp of passion as he fondled her.

"I want you, John," she said. "I want you to take me."

She was still holding his manhood. She brought it to her opening and settled down on it, filling herself with the long, thick pole. If there was any taking going on, Slocum thought as the delicious sensations tried to overwhelm him, Rose was the one doing it.

Then he gave himself over to the flood of feeling and let it wash him away. His hips moved instinctively, driving his shaft in and out of her. Her hands clutched at his chest and she let out a moan. Slocum reached up and cupped her right breast with his left hand, feeling the hard nipple jutting against his palm through her dress, while his right hand slid behind her neck and drew her face down to his. His mouth found hers, his tongue thrusting through her lips to invade the warm, wet cavern beyond. She matched him, her tongue dueling with his, her hips meeting his thrust for thrust.

The intensity of their lovemaking was such that neither of them could withstand it for very long. Slocum dropped his hands to the swell of her hips and held her tightly against him as he drove into her one last time and then stayed there, buried to the hilt. Shudders ran through him as he poured his seed into her in a series of blistering jets. Rose trembled and cried out as her own climax gripped her at the same moment.

Sated, filled to overflowing, she sagged against his broad chest. Both of them were breathing hard, trying to regain the breath they had spent in their exertions. Rose laughed softly and said, "Oh, John. That was so good."

"Yeah," he agreed. "Mighty good."

She lifted her head and reached up to run her fingers along the line of his jaw. "You're a fine man, John Slocum."

He thought about all the blood and death in his past, the bank robberies and stage holdups and all the other times he had skirted the law. "Maybe not as good as you think," he said.

"Good enough for me. I want to tell you—"

The baby let out a loud, lusty yell.

Rose slid out of Slocum's arms, hurriedly rearranging her clothes and then reaching out to pick up the boy. She brought him to her chest and rested his head on her shoulder, bouncing him up and down slightly as she said, "There, there. It's all right, Edgar. It's all right."

Under the topmost buffalo robe, Slocum buttoned up his trousers, thinking that ol' Edgar didn't have the best timing in the world. On the other hand, it could have been worse.

"I'm going to take a look around outside," he told Rose as he pushed the robes aside and stood up.

"Be careful," she said.

"There's nothing out there to worry about," he assured her. "I'll just check on the horses." Mainly, he just needed to relieve himself.

The clouds had thinned some overhead, he saw as he stepped out of the tent and looked up. A few stars were peeking through the overcast here and there. The wind had died down a little too. The floor of the gully was dusted with a thin layer of snow and sleet. The ice crystals crunched under Slocum's boots as he walked over to see if the horses and mules were all right. They seemed to be, although the dun turned its head and gave him a reproachful look, as if wondering why Slocum had subjected it to this miserably cold weather. Slocum laughed quietly and patted the horse on the shoulder, then moved off down the gully to take a leak.

When he got back to the tent, he found that Rose had quieted the baby. Edgar was sleeping again. She had a way with him, Slocum thought. She might not be the boy's mother, but her maternal instincts were good.

"It'll be dawn in a couple of hours," he told her. "We'll get started to Tascosa as soon as we've eaten some breakfast. There's a little bacon and a couple of biscuits left."

"All right," Rose said with a nod of agreement. "What will we do until then?"

"Well, I reckon you could get some more sleep," Slocum suggested.

Her hands went to the buttons of her dress. "I have a better idea. It's too cold to get completely undressed, but I think we could get a few less clothes between us."

Slocum went to her with a smile.

He wound up dozing off anyway, after they had made love again. He went to sleep thinking about how her nipple had tasted when he sucked the hard nubbin and the crinkled ring of brown flesh around it into his mouth.

When he woke up in the morning, Rose was gone, and the baby with her.

3

"Son of a bitch!" Slocum slammed his hat to the ground in frustration after running out of the tent and looking around the gully. He had hoped that Rose had taken Edgar and stepped outside for some reason, but there was no sign of them anywhere he could see. Not only that, but Rose's horse was gone.

Along with Slocum's lineback dun.

He picked up his hat and jammed it on his head, turning the air blue with his curses as he did so. He wasn't sure who he was most angry with: Rose for running off and stealing his horse, or himself for sleeping right through her treachery. She must have bundled Edgar back into the pouch and attached it to the saddle of one of the horses, then led both animals a good long way down the gully before mounting up and riding away. Otherwise, he would have heard the hoofbeats and awakened.

Along with the dun, she had taken what few supplies he had left, as well as what had been inside the tent. The mules and the wagon that had belonged to the dead buffalo hunters were still here, so at least he wasn't completely stranded, Slocum thought. Being set afoot in this weather, this far from town, would have been the same thing as a death sentence. He was glad Rose hadn't done that to him.

The partial clearing of the sky he had observed a few hours

earlier was gone now. The clouds had thickened again into a low, gray ceiling over the plains. More flakes of snow drifted down in occasional flurries.

Slocum looked for tracks in the snow that had already fallen and found them easily enough. They told him that Rose had set off along the gully to the east. That was the opposite direction from Santa Fe. Maybe she had never meant to go to New Mexico Territory in the first place. Maybe that had been another lie. Slocum didn't know what she was capable of. But he was finding out, he told himself grimly.

He struck the tent and loaded it into the back of the wagon, which had a canvas cover fastened over it. Then he hitched up the mules and prodded them into motion with yells and a short whip he found under the wagon seat. The vehicle lurched along the rough bottom of the gully. Slocum kept an eye on the tracks Rose had left in the snow as she fled. He wasn't sure he could catch up to her, since she was on horseback and he was driving this unwieldy wagon, but he was sure going to try. Nobody made a fool out of John Slocum.

And in the back of his mind, he had to reluctantly admit that he was still a mite worried about Rose and Edgar, no matter what the lovely blonde had done to him. He didn't want either of them freezing to death out here on the prairie.

Rose had ridden out of the gully about a mile from the campsite, on the south side of the slash in the earth. The walls were too steep here for the wagon to negotiate, so Slocum had to travel on another half mile or so before he could drive out of the gully and then backtrack to the spot where Rose had left it. He picked up the trail again. Despite Rose's seeming reluctance the night before to go to Tascosa, that seemed to be where she was headed now. The tracks led almost due south.

Slocum shivered inside his coat as the frigid wind blew at his back. People who thought of Texas as having a warm, sunny climate year round had never been in the Panhandle during a blue norther. Slocum had suffered through much worse winters in Wyoming, Montana, Idaho, and the Dakotas, of course, but this was bad enough. His toes felt like chunks of ice inside his boots. The actual temperature was well below freezing, and the wind made it feel even colder.

Given those conditions, Slocum wasn't surprised that he seemed to be alone on the plains. Only a damned fool would be traveling in weather like this, he told himself. He figured he fit that description just fine, the way Rose had taken him in.

The snow became heavier, making it more difficult for Slocum to see the tracks he was following. The horizon in front of him blurred and became indistinct due to the swirling clouds of white flakes in the air. Slocum drove hunched over on the seat, peering narrow-eyed at the impressions left in the snow and ice by the hooves of the horses. Those tracks were filling up with the new snowfall, and Slocum knew that unless he found Rose soon, the trail was going to be gone.

He was so intent on following the tracks that he didn't see the men in front of him until he was almost on top of them. One of the riders let out an angry yell. Slocum's head jerked up and he saw four horsebackers, sitting their mounts side by side so that his path was blocked. They wore buffalo coats and had Sharps carbines cradled in their arms. Slocum hauled back on the reins so that the mules wouldn't run into them.

More buffalo hunters. Right away, Slocum didn't have a good feeling about this.

"Stay right where you are, mister!" one of the men shouted over the howl of the wind. "Who are you?"

"Mighty cold out here for introductions!" Slocum yelled back.

The man moved his rifle so that the big, ugly mouth of the Sharps muzzle was pointed in Slocum's general direction. "I asked you a question!"

"Name's John Slocum! What do you want?"

The man ignored Slocum's question. The other riders were splitting up, moving their horses so that they flanked the wagon. Slocum didn't like that. They were surrounding him.

His Colt was under the sheepskin jacket, and the jacket was

closed. Not only that, but Slocum had pulled his gloves on earlier to keep his fingers from freezing off. He was in no position to start a gunfight.

That wouldn't stop the buffalo hunters. They all wore gloves with the trigger fingers cut out, so they could use their rifles. That wasn't a bad idea, Slocum thought. He might give it a try himself—if he lived through this confrontation.

"Where'd you get this wagon?" the spokesman for the group demanded.

"What business is that of yours?" Slocum shot right back. The odds might be against him, but he wasn't going to back down.

"I know this wagon," the buffalo hunter said. "It belongs to some friends of ours. We came out here lookin' for 'em, since they didn't come into town when this bad weather hit."

Slocum shook his head. "I don't know anything about that," he lied. "My horse stepped in a hole and broke its leg. I would've froze to death out here if I hadn't found this wagon and mule team a little later. They'd been abandoned, so I took them and decided to try to make Tascosa."

It was a thin story, mighty thin, but plausible enough that it could have been true. The fact that Slocum didn't have a saddle horse gave the lie a little weight.

"You sayin' there was nobody with this wagon?" asked one of the other hunters.

"That's right," Slocum insisted. "I looked around and hollered, but there was nobody anywhere close. If something happened to your friends, I'm sorry, but I didn't have anything to do with it."

From the looks of the men, they didn't believe him. Slocum hadn't really expected them to. Spinning that yarn about finding the wagon and the mules had been a longshot, which sometimes paid off. Apparently, this time it wasn't going to, because another of the men said harshly, "This bastard's lyin', Mace. He's done kilt Green and Harper and Keever and stole their wagon."

The first man nodded. "I think so too, Burt."

He was about to get shot to doll rags, Slocum thought. But before he died he was going to do his damnedest to haul out his Colt Navy and take some of his killers to hell with him. Despite what Rose had done, he hoped that she and Edgar would be all right.

The wind suddenly died down, and Slocum heard hoofbeats close by. A new voice called out. The buffalo hunters turned to look, and so did Slocum.

Two more men dressed in thick coats and pulled-down hats rode up to the group. The lower halves of their faces had scarves wrapped around them to protect them from the wind. One of the newcomers said, "Howdy, Mace. Is this the wagon you brought us out here to look for?"

"That's right," Mace said with a curt nod. "We figure this son of a bitch killed Green and his pards and stole the wagon."

The second of the men who had just ridden up said, "It's pure dumb luck you ran across him in this storm. Billy and me were just looking for you so's we could tell you we're heading back to Tascosa."

"All right, Bat," replied Mace. He shot Slocum a venomous glance. "We've found what we were lookin' for anyway."

Slocum wasn't paying much attention to Mace and the other buffalo hunters anymore. At the mention of the name Bat, he had transferred his gaze to the two newcomers, and now he said, "Bat? Bat Masterson? That you and Billy Dixon?"

The second man pulled down his scarf, revealing a familiar face. "Slocum?" he asked.

Slocum nodded. "It's me, all right. Haven't seen you boys in a couple of years. I'm a little surprised you're still down here in the Panhandle."

Bat Masterson pulled down his own scarf, revealing a handsome, mustachioed face. "Hello, John," he greeted Slocum. "You caught us just at the right time. Most of the buffalo are gone, so we're leaving too. I'm for Kansas as soon as this storm is over."

Mace was looking back and forth between Slocum and Bat Masterson and Billy Dixon. "Wait just a damned minute!" he sputtered. "Are you sayin' you know this murderin' thief, Masterson?"

Bat nodded. "Indeed we do. He was at Adobe Walls with us a couple of years ago."

Slocum mustered up a grin and said, "Lot of water under the bridge since then."

"Not enough to make us forget Adobe Walls," Billy Dixon said.

None of the men who had been at Adobe Walls were likely to forget it, Slocum thought. He'd been doing a little buffalo hunting himself at the time, and along with less than forty other men, he had spent nearly a week hunkered behind the walls of the primitive settlement's buildings, besieged by what had looked like thousands of Indians led by the war chief Quanah. Comanche, Kiowa, Arapaho, Cheyenne—they had all come together in an attempt to drive the white hunters from the Panhandle before the slaughter of the buffalo was complete. The siege at Adobe Walls had broken the back of that thrust before it ever got started good, because the hunters holed up inside the settlement had stood off the attacking horde, doing incredible damage with their high-caliber rifles and their deadly accuracy. Quanah's army had finally given up and ridden away, and the legend of Adobe Walls had rapidly spread across the plains.

Now Mace said in a surly voice, "Just because this fella was at Adobe Walls don't mean he didn't kill Green and the others and steal their wagon."

"John Slocum's not a murderer," Bat said coldly. "He's no saint, but I never knew him to kill anybody who didn't need killing."

"Are you sayin' you're standin' up for him?" demanded Mace.

Bat edged his horse closer to the wagon, and Billy followed suit. "That's exactly what I'm saying," Bat responded to Mace's challenge.

The odds still favored Mace and his friends, but now they were a lot closer to even. And Bat Masterson had a growing reputation as a gunman. Slocum had heard how Bat had shot it out with an army sergeant over in Mobeetie after the soldier had ambushed him in an argument over a girl. Billy Dixon was also known as a tough man and a crack shot. Mace and the other buffalo hunters were casting nervous glances back and forth among themselves. Clearly they didn't want to tangle with Bat and Billy, no matter how convinced they were that Slocum had killed their friends and stolen the wagon.

One of the men finally spoke up. "I reckon it could've happened the way this fella said, Mace."

"You mean about findin' the wagon abandoned?" Mace asked.

The hunter swallowed hard and nodded. "Sure. Maybe somethin' else happened to Green and Harper and Keever."

Mace nodded slowly. "I reckon so." He didn't believe it, Slocum could tell, but by pretending to believe Slocum's story, Mace could at least save a little of his dignity.

Billy Dixon said, "We'd better all head for Tascosa, else this blizzard's goin' to freeze us and blow us all away."

"What about Green and the others?" asked Mace.

Bat shook his head. "Whatever happened to them, there's nothing we can do for them now. And I'm not willing to die over it."

Neither were any of the other men. Grudgingly, they all turned their horses south. Mace and the others pulled ahead, but Bat and Billy rode alongside the wagon as Slocum drove.

Slocum nodded toward the disappearing riders in front of them. "What are the chances they'll ride ahead a ways, then stop and set up an ambush?"

"Not likely," Bat said with a chuckle. "They know if they did that, they'd have to kill all three of us. If any of us was left alive, we'd spend the rest of our days hunting them down if we had to, and Mace and his boys know that. Mace is really the only one crazy enough to even consider it, and the others will talk him out of it."

"Mace and that fella Green hunted together for a while," Billy Dixon said. "I reckon Mace feels like he has to stick up for Green.'' Billy spat off to the side. ''But I never saw a sorrier specimen in my life. Green was a no-account, and so were Harper and Keever. If they're out here somewhere froze to death, then I say good riddance.''

Well, they didn't freeze to death, Slocum thought, but by now their corpses were probably good and hard. He kept the notion to himself and didn't say anything about it to Bat and Billy.

He was more interested in finding out something else. ''While you were out here looking for those men, did you see anything of a woman with two horses?''

Bat looked sharply at him. ''A woman? Out in this blue norther? Not very likely, John.''

''I was trailing her,'' Slocum said. He gestured at the ground, carpeted now with a layer of fresh snow. ''The tracks got covered up, though.''

''We're not that far from Tascosa,'' Billy commented. ''Maybe she made it there before the worst of the storm caught up with her. Could be you'll find her waiting for you when we get to town.''

Slocum nodded. That was possible. Rose wouldn't really be waiting for him, of course. She probably thought she would never see him again.

But she was in for a surprise, because Slocum still intended to find her, one way or another. No matter how long it took.

4

Texas cattlemen were beginning to get the idea that if the high plains of the Panhandle were good enough graze for the vast herds of buffalo, they would probably support cattle too. Colonel Ranald Mackenzie's destruction of the Comanche villages in Palo Duro Canyon, along with the slaughtering of the Indians' horse herd, had broken their grip on this part of the country. In the two years since that battle, ranchers had begun to drive their stock up from the south and lay claim to millions of acres. Slocum had heard that Charley Goodnight had established a vast ranch called the J.A. in the canyon itself, covering parts of six counties. Other cattlemen were following the lead of the canny Goodnight, and that meant settlements such as Buffalo Springs, Coldwater, and Tascosa were springing up to serve the needs of the ranchers and the cowboys who rode for their brands.

That meant saloons and whorehouses, and Tascosa had plenty of both.

The weather had driven most folks indoors, Slocum saw as he drove the wagon down the settlement's single street in company with Bat Masterson and Billy Dixon. Only a few people were out and about, and they were bundled up tightly against the chill. Warm yellow light shone from the windows of the buildings they passed. Most of the cowboys in the area would

be on their home ranches waiting out the storm, leaving in
Tascosa only the owners of the various businesses, some buffalo hunters who had waited too late to start back to Dodge
City, and a few hapless travelers who had taken refuge here
from the blue norther.

Slocum figured he fell into that last category.

There were only a handful of horses tied at the hitch rails
along the street. Anybody with any sense who had ridden into
town would have stabled their mounts. Slocum checked the
horses anyway, looking for the dun and Rose's chestnut mare.
He saw no sign of them anywhere, which didn't mean they
weren't already in stalls in one of the town's livery stables, of
which there appeared to be two. Bat and Billy turned toward
the first one they came to, and Slocum followed their lead.

Billy swung down from his saddle and opened the big double doors of the livery barn. Bat rode inside, followed by Slocum in the wagon. Billy led his horse in and shut the doors
behind them. A lantern was hung on a nail driven in the wall
beside the office door. A skinny old-timer with a grizzled
beard, a gimpy leg, and a hat with a pushed-up brim limped
out of the office and greeted them by saying, "What the hell
are you tryin' to do, let all the cold air in?"

Bat grinned at the old man as he dismounted. "Just needed
a place to get in out of the storm, Pete," he said. "Think you
can accommodate us?"

Grudgingly, the stable keeper said, "Well, seein' as it's you,
Bat, I reckon I can find room for your hosses." He cast a
jaundiced eye at Slocum. "This here a friend of your'n?"

"That's right," Bat said. "Pete, meet John Slocum. John,
this is Pete Sawyer."

Slocum jumped down from the wagon, feeling painful tin-
gles go through his half-frozen toes as his booted feet struck
the hard-packed dirt of the stable floor. He held out his hand
and shook with Sawyer. "Got room for the wagon too?" Slocum asked.

"Out back, I reckon—if you can pay."

Slocum dug out a coin, unsure if it was the same five-dollar gold piece he had used to distract the buffalo hunters in the gully or the other one he had been carrying. He flipped it to Sawyer and asked, ''That cover me for a few days?''

The old man bit into the coin and nodded in approval as he studied the marks his teeth had made. ''That'll do,'' he said. ''I'll let you know when it runs out, if you're here that long. You'll have to unhitch your own team. My hostler's sick with the grippe.''

Slocum gestured at the coin. ''Will that buy me something else?''

''What do you mean?'' Sawyer asked with a suspicious frown.

''Information,'' said Slocum. ''Has a woman with a baby and two horses, a dun and a chestnut, showed up here today?''

Sawyer shook his head. ''Not in my stable, they ain't.'' He waved a hand at the stalls. ''Feel free to look around if'n you don't believe me. What would a woman be doin' out here in the middle o' nowhere with a kid?''

That was a question Slocum still couldn't answer, so he didn't even try. He just said, ''Much obliged,'' and turned to Bat Masterson and Billy Dixon, who had unsaddled their horses and put them away in a couple of stalls. ''Give me a hand with those mules?'' Slocum asked.

''I never was much of a hand with mules,'' Bat replied with a grin. ''But Billy seems to communicate with them quite well.''

''You ought to speak their language just fine, you bein' a jackass too,'' Billy said dryly. His smile took any insult out of the words.

Within a few minutes, Slocum and Billy had the mules un-hitched and had rolled the wagon out the back door of the stable into a fenced yard that was usually used for riding stock. In weather like this, though, all the animals were inside the barn.

As he and Billy walked back through the stable and rejoined Bat, Slocum put his hand in his pocket and closed his hand around the remaining coin he found there. That five dollars would buy him a drink, a hot meal, and maybe a chair in a poker game, if he was lucky. From there, he would have to run what was left into a more sizable stake, but he had no doubt he could do it.

Walking between Slocum and Billy Dixon, Bat clapped both of them on the shoulder. "What say we go down to the Deuces and have a drink, maybe sit in on a friendly game of chance?"

That sounded good to Slocum and he said as much. "First, though," he added, "I want to check the other livery stable and see if that woman's been there."

"Ah, yes, the mysterious lady." Bat grinned. "You're going to have to tell us all about her, John."

There wasn't much he *could* tell them, Slocum realized. For all he knew, Rose Delaney wasn't even her real name. She could have been lying about the baby's name too, and even whether or not she was his mother. She had certainly cared for the boy with the solicitude and gentleness of a mother.

Slocum and his two companions turned in at the second livery stable. The bald-headed man running it claimed he hadn't seen a woman in weeks except for the whores who worked in Tascosa's saloons. His two hostlers agreed with him. Slocum wasn't sure whether to believe them or not; there was something shifty about the way the bald-headed man looked at him. But he could see into all the stalls in the barn, and his dun and Rose's chestnut were nowhere to be seen.

What had happened to Rose and Edgar? Slocum couldn't answer that question. Maybe they had missed Tascosa in the storm, skirting the settlement without ever knowing it was there. Maybe Rose had avoided the town on purpose, though that seemed like an awfully chancy thing to do in this weather. South of Tascosa, Rose might find an isolated ranch house where she could seek shelter, but Slocum wouldn't have wanted to bet even his own life on such a possibility, let alone the life of an innocent child.

There was nothing he could do until the situation improved. This storm would blow itself out in a day or two. The cold weather might linger, but once the snow stopped he could move on again. He wasn't sure how he would go about picking up Rose's trail, but he would think of something, he told himself as he accompanied Bat and Billy to the Deuces Saloon.

The wooden doors behind the bat wings were closed against the cold wind. Bat opened them and stepped inside, followed by Slocum and Billy. Bat looked over his shoulder and asked, "Have you been to Tascosa before, John?"

Slocum shook his head. "Not until today. I just know the place by reputation."

"Then you may not know how this establishment got its name. The owner won it in a poker game by bluffing out the competition with nothing more than a pair of deuces. She renamed the saloon in celebration of her win."

"She?" Slocum repeated.

"Our hostess." Bat waved a hand at the bar. "The lovely Arabella."

Slocum followed Bat's gaze to the woman who stood at the end of the bar. She was tall and slender, and the high-necked gown she wore might cover her up, but did little to actually conceal the sensuous curves of her body. Her raven hair was piled high on her head in an elaborate arrangement of curls. She wasn't classically beautiful; her mouth was a little too generous and her jawline a touch too strong for that. But Slocum was immediately drawn to her anyway, and when she turned her head and her eyes met his squarely and directly, he saw an answering flash of interest.

Bat led the way over to the bar and gave the woman a hug and a kiss on the cheek. She was almost as tall as he was, and when she turned to Slocum, she had to tip her head back only slightly to meet his gaze. A soft, slow smile curved her lips as she said, "Hello."

Bat made the introductions. "John Slocum, Miss Arabella Winthrop. Arabella, my good friend John."

"Lady Arabella actually," she said as she extended a hand to Slocum. He took it, finding her fingers cool and strong despite their slenderness. There was only a faint trace of an accent in her voice.

"I'd ask how a British noblewoman wound up running a saloon in a cow town like Tascosa . . ." Slocum began.

"But it's a long, dreadfully boring story," Arabella finished. "If you're ever feeling exceptionally tolerant someday, perhaps I'll tell it to you."

"I'll look forward to it," Slocum said. "Right now I'll settle for a cup of hot coffee with a healthy slug of whiskey in it."

"That can be arranged." Arabella turned to the bartender and said, "Coffee for this gentleman, Phil, with a generous splash of my private stock in it, please."

"Comin' right up, Miss Arabella," Phil said.

Private stock, Slocum thought. He would believe that when he tasted it. No matter what the label on the bottle said, he fully expected what went in his coffee to be typical bar whiskey, the sort of panther piss typically brewed in a bathtub with gunpowder and rattlesnake venom for taste.

Instead, when he tried the coffee Phil put in front of him, he found it to be both smooth and potent. The steaming coffee warmed his hands as he wrapped them around the cup, and the whiskey started a pleasant fire burning in his belly.

Phil brought coffee laced with the same stuff for Bat and Billy. Then Bat asked, "How about some food? John has the look of a hungry man about him, wouldn't you say?"

Arabella nodded. "Definitely hungry." Her smile was bolder, more flirtatious now.

Billy Dixon grunted and went off to sit at one of the tables and watch a poker game. He was a good man, Slocum knew, probably the best scout and the best shot in these parts, but he hadn't been blessed with Bat Masterson's colorful personality. Now that Bat had opened his coat in the warmth of the saloon, Slocum saw that he was wearing a short *charro* jacket such as Mexican *vaqueros* preferred, as well as a scarlet sash tied around his waist. His flat-crowned black hat had a band made of bright studs around it. Bat had a growing reputation not only as a shootist, but also as a dandy.

"I could do with something to eat," Slocum admitted. Arabella told him to go over to one of the empty tables, and it was only a few minutes before a redhead in a low-cut spangled dress brought him a steaming bowl full of stew, along with a couple of thick chunks of bread. Slocum accepted the food with a grateful smile, and the redhead gave him a brazen grin in return. Tascosa was a right friendly place, he decided.

Bat was still at the bar talking to Arabella. As Slocum ate hungrily, he watched them from the corner of his eye, wondering if there was anything between Bat and the beautiful British saloonkeeper. From the way Bat was joshing with her, there didn't appear to be anything romantic there, but if Slocum did decide to see if Arabella would be interested in the pleasure of his company—so to speak—he would ask Bat first if it was all right. The way Slocum saw it, he owed his life to Bat and Billy Dixon, because Mace and the other buffalo hunters would have no doubt blasted him to hell with those Sharps rifles of theirs if Bat and Billy hadn't ridden up when they did.

The whiskey in the coffee counteracted any effect the strong black brew might have had otherwise, making Slocum drowsy. Filling his belly with hot food had the same result. He had chosen a table where he could sit with his back to the wall—an old habit that he had no desire to break—so after he finished eating he leaned his chair back and tugged his hat down over his eyes. With few cowboys in town, the Deuces wasn't busy, so there wasn't a great deal of noise in the saloon. A little talk, the soft slap of cards on felt, a woman's quiet laugh, the hissing of kerosene lamps . . . all those sounds combined into a lullaby for Slocum, who could have let himself drift off to sleep quite easily.

Instead, a movement outside, barely glimpsed through the fogged-over window, made him sit up alertly. The day was still gray and gloomy, and the condensation on the glass made it even more difficult to tell what he was seeing. Alarm bells were going off in the back of Slocum's brain, however, so he stood up and stepped over to the big front window to the side of the saloon's entrance. Behind him, Bat called out, "John? What is it?"

Slocum lifted a hand and rubbed it over the glass, clearing away most of the moisture but leaving some streaks behind that fragmented the scene he was seeing and made it look like some kid's puzzle. He frowned as he peered at the buildings across the deserted street.

Then something moved again and he saw the barrel of a rifle protruding around the corner of a building. Whoever was holding it was in an alley, hidden by a rain barrel. But as Slocum's eyes widened in shock, he had no doubt where the rifle was aimed.

Red fire geysered from the weapon's muzzle, sending a bullet right at him.

5

Slocum threw himself backward, letting instincts honed by long years of riding in the path of danger take over. As he fell, the window shattered. Jagged slivers of glass showered over Slocum as he sprawled on the sawdust-littered floor. One of the splinters opened a shallow cut on the palm of his left hand as he shielded his face with it.

Frightened screams and angry shouts filled the smoky air of the Deuces. Cold air blew in through the broken window, making the flames in the kerosene lanterns flicker and dance wildly. Slocum rolled over and came up on his knees, ignoring the pieces of broken glass that poked painfully through his jeans. He yanked the Colt Navy from its holster and crouched at the window. He thrust the barrel of the gun through the opening made by the bushwhacker's rifle slug and started triggering toward the alley across the street. When the Colt was empty, he flattened himself on the floor again and dug under his coat for fresh cartridges. A glance over his shoulder told him that everyone else in the saloon had sought shelter too. High-powered rifle bullets could punch right through the clapboard walls of the building, and from the sound of the shot Slocum had heard, the ambusher was using a buffalo gun.

No more shots had come from across the street after the first one, however, and after a moment, Bat Masterson called out to Slocum, "Maybe whoever it was took off for the tall and uncut, John."

"Seems that way, but I don't reckon I'm willing to bet my life on it just yet," replied Slocum. His Colt was reloaded by now, and he held it tightly as he rose for a cautious look through the broken window, ready to return fire if he saw anything the least bit suspicious.

Instead he saw a tall, brawny man in a high-crowned hat stalking down the street carrying a shotgun. The man walked right out in the open, as if daring anybody to shoot at him. Slocum called, "Bat, come here and see if you know who this gent is."

Bat joined Slocum at the window and peered out at the man coming toward the saloon. He squinted against the cold wind. "That's Cape Williamson, the local sheriff," Bat said. "A good man, John. Nobody's going to take any potshots at you while Cape's around."

Slocum nodded. He holstered his gun and stood up as Sheriff Williamson's boot heels rang on the porch of the saloon. The lawman jerked open the door and strode into the Deuces. "What's going on here?" he demanded in a loud voice.

Arabella came forward, moving smoothly through the small crowd that parted before her. "Someone took a shot at my establishment, Sheriff," she said. "The bullet broke out that window, as you can see."

"I heard more than one shot," Williamson pointed out. "Sounded like a war down here for a minute. Somebody emptied a six-gun."

Slocum stepped forward. "That'd be me. I'm the one the bushwhacker was after. Thought it might be a good idea to make him hunt some cover."

Williamson regarded him with narrowed eyes. "And who might you be, mister?" he asked.

"Name's John Slocum." Maybe Williamson wouldn't recognize the name from any old reward dodgers, Slocum hoped, but that was always a possibility. He had broken the law a few times, no use denying it, and had been blamed for even more crimes that he hadn't committed. Still, there was no point in lying about his name. Too many people in Tascosa already knew it.

Bat spoke up, saying, "He's a friend of mine, Sheriff."

Williamson grunted. "Are you vouching for him, Masterson, or trying to get him in trouble by telling me that?"

Bat put a hand over his heart and grinned. "Why, Sheriff! You wound me deeply. You know I'm a law-abiding man."

"Then why don't you take that deputy's job I've offered you?" Williamson demanded.

"I've thought about it," Bat answered seriously. "Maybe I will carry a badge one of these days. But right now I just want to get back up to Kansas when the weather clears."

Williamson turned back to Slocum. "You see where the shot came from?"

"The alley across the street," Slocum said, "between those two buildings." He pointed through the broken window to indicate which buildings he was talking about. "I saw the barrel poking out and ducked just in time."

The lawman studied the window, which was still fogged up inside. After a moment, he said, "How did some bushwhacker even know you were in here, Slocum? Nobody could see through that window from outside."

That same question had already occurred to Slocum. Maybe he had jumped to a conclusion he shouldn't have. He turned his head to look at something, then strode over to the table where he had been sitting. He put his finger on a hole in the wall. "That's where the bullet wound up," he said. "And that's where I was sitting."

"So whoever took that shot knew you were sitting there and just aimed to put his bullet in the general vicinity?" Williamson sounded dubious, but it was the only explanation that made any sense.

Slocum nodded. "That means he was either in here and saw where I was sitting just before he took the shot, or somebody else told him where to aim."

"You see anybody leave out of here just before the shooting

started?'' asked Williamson. At least he was considering the theory as a possibility, Slocum thought.

"Not really," Slocum said. "I wasn't paying that much attention. The place wasn't real busy, but people were going in and out pretty regular."

"I saw somebody leave," said Billy Dixon, causing the others to turn and look at him. He had resumed his seat at one of the tables, but he pushed himself to his feet and came over to join Slocum, Bat, Sheriff Williamson, and Arabella. "It was one of those buffalo hunters," Billy went on, "the one called Burt. He rides with Mace Jones."

That explained a lot, thought Slocum. Even though Mace and the other hunters had backed down earlier in the day, they probably still thought that Slocum was responsible for the deaths of their friends. And of course they were right, though Slocum had killed Green and Harper and Keever to save his own life and that of Rose Delaney. Only someone who placed a high estimation on his accuracy would attempt to target a specific individual through a fogged-over window—but Slocum could imagine Mace doing just that.

"I'll go over and take a look at that alley," Sheriff Williamson said. "I don't expect to find much, though."

"We'll go with you," Bat said. "John, you walk in the middle, just so Mace can't get a good shot at you if he's still skulking around."

"Just hold on," said Williamson. "You don't know Jones is the one who shot at Slocum. You shouldn't ought to go accusing somebody without proof, Masterson."

"Well, let's go take a look," Bat suggested.

But just as Williamson had predicted and Slocum had suspected, there was nothing in the alley to indicate who had fired the shot. The snow had been disturbed by someone who left behind a welter of footprints, but there was nothing distinctive about the tracks. Anybody wearing boots could have made them. Nor were there any spent cartridges lying in the snow.

Slocum had halfway hoped to see a splash of blood on the ground, indicating that at least one of his wild shots had found its mark, but there was no blood to be seen. The bushwhacker had escaped unhurt.

Which meant that he could try again, whenever the notion took him.

That same thought must have occurred to the sheriff, because Williamson looked at Slocum and asked, "You got a place to stay while you wait out the storm?"

"Not yet."

"Better find one. Someplace you can hunker down. I don't want no killings in my town."

"Neither do I, Sheriff," Slocum said dryly.

Bat put a hand on Slocum's arm. He and Billy Dixon had accompanied Slocum and Williamson over to the alley. "Come on, John," Bat said. "I'm willing to bet you can get a room at Arabella's."

That sounded promising. Slocum went back across the street with Bat and Billy while Williamson stomped off through the snow to his office.

Some canvas had been fastened across the broken window to block the wind that had been whipping through the hole. Slocum, Bat, and Billy found Arabella standing at the bar, a wistful expression on her face as she looked at the shattered pane.

"Do you know how much it cost to have that window freighted out here from Fort Worth?" she asked.

Slocum shook his head. "No, but I'm sorry it got busted because of me, Lady Arabella. I'd offer to pay to have it replaced, but I'm a mite short on funds right now."

Arabella shook her head and waved off Slocum's apology. "Oh, no, don't worry about it, Mr. Slocum. Bullet holes are an occupational hazard when you're the proprietor of a saloon. This isn't the first time someone has opened fire on the Deuces."

"But Jones, or whoever that bushwhacker was, aimed to kill *me*. That makes it personal."

Bat leaned on the bar and said, "Chances are, Mace and

his boys took off and won't be back. They just took one last try at you before riding on, John.''

Slocum frowned. He thought Bat was being overly optimistic. Weather like this made it difficult to travel, so Mace was probably still somewhere around Tascosa. Slocum was going to have to be careful and watch his back at all times.

That was going to make it more difficult to find Rose and the baby, but Slocum hadn't given up on that. He wanted that dun horse back, but even more, he wanted to know why Rose had run off like that.

"Bat said you might have a place where I could stay until the weather clears," Slocum told Arabella. "I can't guarantee I can pay you for a room, and after everything that's happened, I don't want to impose on your hospitality—"

"Nonsense," she said briskly. "There are vacant rooms upstairs, and I see no point in letting them go to waste. You're welcome to stay, Mr. Slocum."

"Call me John."

"Of course . . . if you'll call me just Arabella."

Slocum was more than willing to do that. The drowsiness he'd felt earlier after finishing the stew and the whiskey-laced coffee had disappeared. Being shot at had a way of waking a fella up, Slocum had long since discovered. He inclined his head toward one of the tables where a poker game was going on and said, "I think I'll sit in for a few hands. Maybe I can win enough to pay my own debts."

"If not, I'll stand good for you, John," Bat offered.

Slocum just nodded. He didn't intend for things to come to that point. Phil drew him a beer, and he carried it over to the table to wait for the hand that was under way to be concluded before taking a vacant chair—once again, with his back to the wall.

The afternoon passed pleasantly and uneventfully. Slocum was able to determine quickly that none of the other players at the table were cheating, which was good. Nothing ruined a friendly game of poker more than having to shoot somebody. He played a cautious game, winning more hands than he lost, and by evening the few dollars he had started with had been transformed into a stake worth almost a hundred bucks. That was more than enough to pay for his own food, drink, and lodging, with some left over to replenish his supplies and pay Arabella for the broken window. When it came time to leave Tascosa, he intended to see if he could trade the mules and wagon to Pete Sawyer for a good horse and saddle. The rig didn't really belong to him, of course, but under the circumstances the former owners wouldn't be showing up to contest any claim he might make.

He didn't see Bat and Billy anywhere around, but Arabella was sitting at one of the tables with a glass of wine at her elbow and some ledger books spread out in front of her. She looked up as Slocum strolled toward the bar and caught his eye. The invitation to join her was plain to see on her striking face. Slocum went over to her table.

"Sit down and have a glass of wine with me, John," Arabella said. "I'll be finished with these figures in a moment."

"It would be my pleasure," Slocum told her truthfully.

She motioned to Phil, who brought over another glass and the bottle of wine. Slocum glanced at the label and saw that the printing was in French, for whatever that was worth. He had never been much of a wine fancier; his tastes ran more to beer and whiskey. But this was good, whatever it was.

"I'll bet you pay a pretty penny to have this stuff freighted in too," Slocum commented as he lowered his glass.

"It's well worth it," said Arabella. "Besides, it won't always be so expensive to live here in Tascosa. When the railroad comes through, the cost of supplies should drop considerably."

"Is the railroad coming this way?"

"Well . . . someday I'm certain it will."

Slocum nodded slowly. He understood what Arabella meant. Folks in these isolated settlements could only hope that someday civilization would extend its reach to them. But to a large extent, their hopes were dependent on forces they could not control. The railroad right-of-way running a mile or so in one direction or the other could mean the difference between one town thriving and growing and another settlement dying on the vine. Slocum had seen many a ghost town that had been bypassed by the rails. He hoped that fate wouldn't someday be in store for Tascosa.

Arabella closed the book in which she had been writing figures. She looked up at Slocum with a smile and said, "There, that's done. It's always a relief to be finished with the ledgers at the end of the month."

"Is it the end of the month?" asked Slocum.

"You don't know what day it is?" Arabella sounded as if she had a hard time believing that.

Slocum shrugged. "I could probably stop and figure it out if I needed to. I didn't pay too much attention to what day it was when I left Pueblo, though." He didn't explain that he'd spent most of his time in the Colorado city in bed with a certain blonde and hadn't given a damn what day it was. "Since then, I've been on the move."

"I see. It's the last day of November."

"I'll try to remember that," Slocum said with a nod. In truth, though, he wouldn't go to that much trouble. Time meant little to him. He was much more concerned with having enough to eat and drink and a pretty woman to share his bed. Throw in a good cigar now and then, a horse he could depend on, and a horizon to beckon him ever onward, and he was a happy man.

"Why don't you have dinner with me?" Arabella said.

"I'd like that." Slocum smiled slowly at her. That flash of interest he had seen in her eyes earlier was still there.

She pushed back her chair and stood up, not waiting on ceremony. "In my room in half an hour," she said. "Go to the top of the stairs and turn left. It's the last door."

Slocum nodded. "I'll be there."

"I'll be expecting you. Don't be late." She turned and walked away, and Slocum watched her go. A long-legged woman ascending a staircase was always a pretty sight, but Arabella made it even more special.

Phil had left the bottle of wine. Slocum picked it up and poured more in his glass, then took a small sip, savoring it. He didn't intend to rush anything tonight.

He had a feeling it would be much better if he took it slow.

6

Slocum knocked on the door and heard Arabella's throaty voice answer from inside, "Come in." He turned the knob and swung the door open.

The big barroom downstairs was furnished functionally, with nothing overly fancy about it. Slocum suspected the other rooms in the Deuces were the same way. But that couldn't be said about Lady Arabella Winthrop's personal quarters. Arabella had obviously spared no expense on them.

The floor was covered with a thick rug, and there were paintings on the walls. Velvet drapes were drawn over the windows. A small fireplace was on the other side of the room, which was warm from the blaze that crackled merrily there. The room was large enough for two dominant pieces of furniture, a large four-poster bed with a silken cover and ruffles around it, and a heavy hardwood table that had been polished to a high shine. Two candles burned on that table in holders that looked like real gold. The table was set with fine china and crystal. In the center of it were platters of roast beef and ham, sweet potatoes, peas, and light, fluffy rolls. It had taken some time to prepare a dinner like this, and Slocum knew that Arabella must have had her cook working on it long before she had asked him to dine with her. She had been pretty sure what his answer would be.

But that didn't bother Slocum. It told him that Arabella was a woman who knew what she wanted—and that she intended to get it.

If there was any doubt about that, the smile with which she greeted Slocum—and the way she was dressed—dispelled it.

She wore a dressing gown of dark blue silk. The neckline plunged dramatically into the valley between her breasts, revealing twin swells of creamy flesh. Her hair was still pinned up, and she managed to look both elegant and sensuous at the same time. She said, "Hello, John. You're right on time."

She came around the table to meet him, with a sway in her walk that was timeless. She took his hat and the sheepskin coat and placed them on a side table. She didn't ask for his gunbelt, which made Slocum trust her even more. In the past, he'd had women try to lure him into taking off his gun with the promise of their bodies, only to have them betray him and set him up for an ambush. Slocum was confident that wasn't what Arabella had in mind for tonight.

"Sit down," she murmured. "I'll pour the wine."

Slocum had drunk two more glasses of wine downstairs, but he was still clearheaded. Wine had never had much of an effect on him, and he was grateful for that now. The last thing he wanted to do was doze off before he and Arabella got down to serious business.

She poured the wine and served the food, and Slocum thought wryly that he could get used to being pampered like this. Not if it meant settling down and staying in one place, though. Nothing was worth that.

But Arabella was enough to make a man reconsider his fiddlefooted ways . . . at least for a minute or two.

The food was excellent, and Slocum thoroughly enjoyed the meal. As they were eating, Arabella said, "I know that it's a breach of frontier etiquette to ask such a question, but I'd really like to know where you're from, John."

He didn't mind telling her. "Georgia, originally."

"Ah, a Southern gentleman!"

Slocum chuckled and said, "Not hardly. I was raised on a

farm, dirt poor most of my life. Never traveled more than five miles from home . . . until the war.''

"You fought for the Confederacy, I'm sure."

He nodded. "I did, and I don't apologize for it. But the war's been over for more than ten years, and I don't hold a grudge against the Yankees. Since coming West, I've run into a lot of good men who fought for the North."

"You didn't go back to your farm after the war was over?"

"I went," Slocum said. "There was nothing there for me."

Nothing but trouble, he added silently to himself. His parents dead and a carpetbagger judge just drooling over the land he intended to take for himself, even though it should have belonged to Slocum. But in those days, in that place, the law had been whatever the corrupt Reconstructionists said it was, so Slocum had fought back the only way he knew how. The only thing that Yankee judge had gotten out of his attempted land grab was a bullet.

And ever since, John Slocum had been on the run from a murder charge that would no doubt haunt him to the end of his days. Slocum could live with that—and die with it too, when his time came.

He didn't say any of that to Arabella, and as if she sensed that she had been probing a sensitive area, she changed the subject. "What brings you to Tascosa?" she asked. "I know you rode in with Bat Masterson and Billy Dixon. Have you been hunting buffalo with them?"

Slocum shook his head. "I've hunted buffalo before, but not lately. I just happened to run into Bat and Billy on my way into town. We've ridden together in the past."

"And they helped you avoid some sort of confrontation with that man Jones and his friends?"

"That's right. What do you know about Mace Jones?"

"I know I don't like him," Arabella said firmly and without hesitation. "I know that the men one is likely to meet in a place such as this would never be at home in an English drawing room. That doesn't bother me, because if I'd wanted that sort of man I could have stayed in England. But Jones and the others . . ." She shook her head. "They're just about the worst lot I've ever seen. I wouldn't put anything past them, John."

"Neither would I. That's why I intend to be careful while I'm here in town."

"An excellent idea. My bartenders and my girls and I will help you in any way we can."

Slocum leaned back in his chair. "You're mighty quick to lend a hand to somebody you just met today," he mused.

"I'm a good judge of character," Arabella said. "A woman in my line of work has to be. I can tell a great deal about you just by looking at you and talking with you."

A smile curved Slocum's mouth. "Is that so? What can you tell?"

"That you're a hard and dangerous man," she replied bluntly, taking him a little by surprise. "You've known more than your share of trouble in your life." Her expression softened as she reached across the table and took hold of his right hand with both of hers. "Yet you haven't allowed it to make you cold and unfeeling. There is still a great deal of warmth in you, John Slocum."

He lifted her right hand, brought it to his mouth, and kissed the back of it. Then he turned it over and pressed his lips to her palm. His tongue circled against her skin. Arabella closed her eyes, tipped her head back, and shivered a little. She swallowed and whispered, "Yes, a great deal of warmth indeed."

Slocum stood up, pushing the chair back with his foot. He drew Arabella with him and stepped around the end of the table so that he could pull her into his arms. She lifted her face to his, her lips already parted for his kiss. His tongue slid hotly into her mouth on a journey of passionate exploration.

Arabella put her arms around his neck and molded her body to his. Slocum felt her breasts flattening against his chest. He put one hand on her back and slid the other down to the swell of her hips, caressing her through the soft silk of the gown. He thrust forward enough so that she could feel the unmistakable evidence of his arousal against the softness of her belly. Her hips began to make slight, involuntary motions of their own, rubbing her pelvis up and down along the hard ridge of male flesh.

Slocum's hand trailed around her flank and then up to her breast, sliding between his body and hers so that he could slip his fingers inside her gown and cup the sensitive globe of flesh. It filled his hand, and his palm scraped over the hard nipple as he began squeezing and kneading. Arabella pushed her groin harder against his and sent her own tongue spearing into his mouth, which rapidly became the site of a fierce, wet duel, a contest with no losers, only winners. Slocum spread her gown apart and moved his caresses to her other breast.

She broke the kiss and said breathlessly, "My God!" Slocum knew what she meant. The need that had gripped them both was incredibly powerful, and he longed to give in to it, to throw her on that fancy four-poster bed and ram his shaft into her like a lust-crazed bull. But he remembered his resolve to take things slow, to make this night special, and he conquered the impulse with a shudder of effort.

He stepped back and spread her gown open even more. As he had suspected, she was naked beneath the silken garment. With most of her body revealed to him, he moved closer again and bent to trail kisses over the hollow of her throat and down onto her breasts. He sucked each nubbin in turn into his mouth, sending sensations through her that made her tangle her fingers in his hair and hold his head close to her. Eventually, Slocum moved on, kissing her belly and reaching between her legs to find her hot, slick core. She gasped as two of his fingers slid into her.

While her hips worked back and forth on his impaling fingers, she reached up with a feverish cry and stripped off the gown, leaving her naked before him. She pulled the pins from her hair and shook her head so that it tumbled in raven waves around her face and down her back. As Slocum buried his face in the triangle of black, fine-spun hair at the juncture of her thighs, she rested her hands on his shoulders and drove herself against him in a frenzy.

"The bed, John!" she said frantically. "Oh, God, the bed!"

Slocum obliged, straightening to his full height and putting his arms around her so that he lifted her as he did so. She clung to him urgently as he moved the few feet to the bed. Not bothering to pull back the cover, Slocum lowered her onto it. She sat on the edge and reached for his belt as he started unbuttoning his shirt.

Trying to take it slow was one thing. Standing up before a veritable avalanche of need was another. Between the two of them, they practically ripped Slocum's clothes off. When he was naked, Arabella lunged for the stiff pole of flesh that jutted out proudly from his groin. She wrapped both hands around it, then lowered her head and sucked the tip of it into her mouth. Slocum groaned as he felt the heat of her tongue swirling around the sensitive flesh. It took all of his self-control not to spill his seed into her mouth right then and there.

Slowly, she swallowed more and more of him until half his length was buried in her mouth. Then she began bobbing up and down, first withdrawing, then engulfing him again until he felt the shudder of approaching climax. He grasped her shoulders and pulled her up. She let out a little cry as his manhood popped out of her clutching mouth.

But then Slocum pressed her back on the bed and her legs opened and she tossed her head from side to side and said, "Yes! Yes!" as he positioned himself and drove into her, filling her with one thrust. He was in her to the hilt, and he held himself there for a moment before launching into the ageless rhythm of man and woman.

Somehow, Slocum kept going as she cried out and clutched wildly at him and her heels beat a mad tattoo on his back. He drove on even as she peaked, his efforts keeping her from sliding back down. Instead she was lifted to even greater heights in a series of cascading explosions. Finally, when Slocum couldn't stand it any longer, he gave in to the need that had gripped him for so long and surged into her, filling her to overflowing with the juices that jetted from him as his climax shook him.

It was as fine a ride as he'd ever had in his life.

For a while after that, Slocum wasn't aware of much of anything. He knew—but only vaguely—that he was lying in Arabella's bed with Arabella snuggled up against his side. His chest heaved up and down as he tried to catch his breath. He stroked her, exploring all the round softnesses of her, while her fingers curled tenderly around his still partially erect shaft.

Slocum looked up at the ceiling and blinked his eyes, trying to force his brain to start working clearly again. A tiny part of him warned him that it wasn't smart to get so lost in the afterglow of lovemaking that he didn't know what was going on around him.

For one thing, where the hell was his gun?

He lifted his head and looked around. He had been in such a rush to get rid of his clothes that he couldn't remember where he had put the Colt Navy. But then he saw his gunbelt coiled on a chair within reach of the bed, and Slocum was glad that even under the circumstances, his instincts had led him to leave the gun where he could reach it in a hurry if he needed to.

Not that he expected that need to arise. Arabella's bartenders and bouncers were downstairs, and Bat Masterson and Billy Dixon were probably somewhere close by too. And there was Sheriff Cape Williamson as well, who had struck Slocum as a hard-nosed lawman who wouldn't allow too much hell-raising in his town. No, in all likelihood, he wouldn't need the Colt tonight.

What he would need was stamina, because Arabella was already pumping her hand up and down on his shaft again, obviously trying to prime it for another bout.

Slocum was game to try.

Arabella decided she had other ideas, though. She leaned over him and gave him a kiss, then said, "I want some more wine. Why don't I bring the glasses over here to the bed?"

Slocum nodded. "Sounds good to me." He didn't particularly care whether he had any more wine or not, but he got to lie back with his head propped up on the pillows and watch appreciatively as Arabella got out of bed and walked over to the table, completely unself-conscious in her nakedness.

She picked up the glasses and the bottle of wine and returned to the bed, her high, firm, coral-tipped breasts bobbing
just slightly as she walked. Smiling, she perched on the edge
of the bed and filled the glasses, then held one of them out
toward Slocum.

"We should drink a toast," she said, "a toast to the two of
us—"

Slocum would have agreed with her, except at that moment
the door of the room crashed open and a man loomed there,
the gun in his hand leveled at the bed. As Slocum's hand
started instinctively toward his own Colt, the gunman said
sharply, "Don't do it, mister! I can't kill you yet, but I can
sure put a bullet in that pretty little lady's head!"

Slocum froze, his hand still a foot away from the Colt Navy.

"That's better," the gunman said. "Now, you bastard,
where the hell's that baby?"

7

The question stunned Slocum, so that for several seconds, all he could do was gape at the man with the gun. Baby? What baby?

Then he remembered Rose Delaney and little Edgar. The boy was the only infant Slocum had been around in a long time. The gunman had to be referring to him.

Slocum wasn't ready to admit that to the stranger, though. He glanced at Arabella. She looked scared, but she wasn't panicking. She was nervy. Slocum supposed a woman in her line of work would have to be. He decided to try to string the gunman along, in the hope that someone downstairs had heard the door of Arabella's room being kicked open.

He wasn't sure how likely that was. The player piano was going strong, even louder than it had been before. Raucous laughter blended with the music. Everybody downstairs was having a fine old time, thought Slocum . . . so fine that maybe he and Arabella were on their own up here.

"I don't know what you're talking about," he told the stranger. "Whatever you're looking for, mister, you've got the wrong room. Now get out of here, and I won't have to kill you."

The man grinned, revealing white, even teeth. He was tall, broad through the shoulders, bulky in a long canvas duster. A broad-brimmed, flat-crowned brown hat sat on a tangle of light brown hair. He was lantern-jawed, not spectacularly ugly but a far cry from being what anyone would call handsome. He kept the gun lined on Arabella and said, "You're lying. You came into town looking for a woman and a baby. You asked about them at both livery stables. That means you know something. Where did you see them last?"

Obviously, this fella had done some asking around of his own, Slocum thought. He wondered suddenly if the man was Rose's husband. If that was the case, then he might have the right to be demanding some answers about the location of his wife and child.

But regardless of what justification the man might have, Slocum had never cottoned to having a gun waved at him. Nor did he like the way the stranger had so callously threatened Arabella.

She was still holding the wine glasses and had made no move to clutch the sheet and hide her nakedness. Slocum might have hoped that the sight of her lovely body would distract the gunman, but he didn't seem to be paying any attention to that. He regarded Arabella as just a lever to get what he wanted out of Slocum.

"This is my place," she said abruptly. "I want you to put that gun away and leave here immediately, sir, or I shall be forced to summon Sheriff Williamson."

A faint grin, the first sign of real emotion from the stranger, tugged at the corners of his mouth for a second. "How are you going to do that, lady?" he asked without taking his eyes off Slocum. "I've got the gun, and nobody knows I'm here. I made sure of that. I came up the back stairs from the alley behind this place, and everybody downstairs is too busy carousing to pay any attention to what's going on up here. Now, I'm getting tired of waiting, mister. I want to know what you know about that baby."

Arabella's voice trembled with justifiable anger as she said, "Don't tell this brute a thing, John. Not one single thing."

"I don't intend to," Slocum said tersely.

The gunman's control slipped for a second. His lips curled in a snarl of impatient anger, and the barrel of the gun in his hand swung slightly toward Slocum. As it did, Arabella made her move, twisting on the edge of the bed and flinging both glasses full of wine as hard as she could at the stranger.

He took an involuntary step backward as the wine splashed over his face and down his chest and the glasses thudded against him. Slocum was already diving off the bed. He had moved at the same instant as Arabella. His hand closed around the butt of the Colt and yanked it from its holster as he fell to the floor and rolled over. He came up on one knee, hoping to hell that Arabella had gotten out of the line of fire.

She had. Slocum saw that as the stranger triggered off a shot. The wine splashing in his eyes had blurred his vision and thrown off his aim, however, and the bullet whipped past Slocum's head to bury itself in the wall behind him. Slocum fired, but the man twisted away and ducked out into the hall, cussing a blue streak as he did so. The clatter of his boots receded rapidly as he ran down the hall. From the way the stranger was moving, Slocum judged that his return shot had missed.

The two gun blasts had finally alerted everyone in the saloon that something was wrong. Heavy footsteps pounded on the stairs. Slocum reached for his pants and jerked them on, glancing at Arabella as he did so. "Are you all right?"

She was crouched on the other side of the bed. She pulled the cover off and wrapped it around her as she nodded. "Go after him, John," she said. "How dare he come in here and threaten us like that!"

Slocum emerged from the room just as Phil reached the top of the stairs with several burly men right behind him. The bartender had a bungstarter clutched in his hand and a worried look on his face. "Miss Arabella—" he began.

"She's all right," Slocum told him. "Did anybody come down that way?"

Phil shook his head. "Nobody got past us. I thought I saw somebody run along the balcony here, though."

"Where are the back stairs?"

"Down at the other end of the hall," Phil said, jerking a thumb in that direction.

Slocum hurried past the bartender. "He came in that way. Chances are he went out the same way."

"Who?" Phil asked from behind Slocum, trotting along to keep up with the drifter's long strides.

"The son of a bitch who busted in on Lady Arabella and me and took a shot at us."

Phil cursed and hurried up alongside Slocum. "You say he came up the back stairs?"

"That's what he claimed."

"There's a man watching that door."

Slocum glanced over at the bartender. He didn't doubt the gunman's story; there was no way the man could have come through the crowded barroom without someone noticing him. But that meant he had somehow gotten past the guard at the back door.

Slocum reached the door at the far end of the hall and jerked it open, revealing a small, square landing. A narrow staircase fell away to the left. The stairwell was illuminated by a kerosene lantern hung on the wall just inside the door. Its light spilled down the stairs to reveal the crumpled shape lying at the bottom.

"Damn it," Phil said as he looked past Slocum and down the stairs, "that's got to be Jasper."

The stairwell was deserted except for the corpse of the murdered guard. The narrow rear door stood wide open, letting in cold air. Slocum winced from the frigid blast as he walked down the stairs, gun held ready just in case the man who had invaded the saloon was still outside, lying in ambush. Even before he reached the bottom, he could see the blood pooling around the head of the crumpled shape.

The first thing Slocum did was reach out, grab the door-knob, and jerk the door closed. That way he wasn't silhouetted against the light from the stairwell as he knelt beside the corpse and rolled it over. As he had suspected, the man's throat had been cut with what looked like a single swipe from a Bowie or another heavy-bladed knife. The big gunman in the duster hadn't wanted to leave anybody behind him to raise the alarm.

"That's Jasper, all right," Phil said as he looked down from the stairs at the dead man's pale, narrow face. "Poor son of a bitch."

Slocum echoed those sentiments mentally. Jasper's features were set in an expression that was a mixture of pained grimace and puzzled frown. He probably hadn't known he was even in danger until someone had looped an arm around his neck, jerked his head back, and sliced that heavy blade across his throat.

Slocum stood up and said to Phil, "Get everybody back to the barroom and send somebody to fetch Sheriff Williamson."

"Likely he heard those shots and is on his way already," the bartender replied. "But I'll make sure of it, Mr. Slocum."

The crowd went back upstairs, down the hall to the balcony, then descended the main staircase. Slocum trailed along behind them, continuing on past the stairs toward Arabella's room. He hadn't seen Bat Masterson or Billy Dixon among the men, and he wondered briefly where they were.

Arabella was fully dressed in a high-necked gown when Slocum came into the room. She turned toward him with an anxious expression and asked, "Are you all right, John? I didn't hear any more shots. What about that man?"

"We didn't find him," Slocum said grimly. "And I've got some bad news for you, Arabella. That fella Jasper, who watches the back stairs for you . . . he's dead."

She put her hand to her mouth and after a moment drew a deep breath, letting it out with a shudder. "I was afraid of that when the man said he'd come in that way. Jasper would never let anyone pass without first making sure that he meant me no harm."

All of Arabella's employees seemed to be devoted to her. Slocum wasn't surprised. She had an air of class about her that would instill loyalty in just about anyone. He said,

"Looked like the stranger jumped Jasper and killed him quick so that he couldn't raise a ruckus. I'm sorry, Arabella."

"It's not your fault," she said dully.

Slocum wasn't so sure about that. If he hadn't started asking questions about Rose and the baby, the trail wouldn't have led here to the Deuces.

But he had never been one to dwell on things he couldn't change, and besides, there had been no way for him to know that a few simple questions would put someone else in danger.

Despite the fire in the fireplace, there was still a chill in the air. Slocum shivered as he pulled the rest of his clothes on. "We'd better go downstairs," he said. "The sheriff ought to be here any minute."

Cape Williamson had already arrived at the Deuces, Slocum saw as he and Arabella descended the stairs to the barroom. The lawman was standing beside the bar talking to Phil, and as he turned toward them, he glowered at Slocum.

"You ride into town and all hell starts breakin' loose," said Williamson. "You must carry trouble around in your hip pocket, mister."

"I didn't invite that son of a bitch to kill a man and take a shot at me," Slocum snapped.

"You ever see him before?"

Slocum shook his head. "Nope."

"What did he want?"

"He was talking like a madman," Arabella said. "He kept asking about a baby."

That made Williamson's frown deepen. "A baby?" he repeated. "You got a kid, Slocum?"

"Not that I know of." Slocum halfway wished that Arabella hadn't said anything about the baby, but given the fact that he had already asked some questions of his own about Rose and the child, there was no point in trying to keep it a secret now.

The sheriff rubbed his jaw in thought. "Maybe this fella got you mixed up with somebody else," he suggested.

"Anything's possible," Slocum said with a shrug.

A couple of men hurried into the saloon, and when Slocum

glanced over at them, he recognized Bat Masterson and Billy Dixon. The two of them came over to the bar, and Bat said, "We heard there was some trouble here. You look like you're all right, though, John."

Slocum nodded. "Came close to getting ventilated, but not quite."

"Damn, I wish I'd been here! Billy and I went down to the stable to check on our horses."

"You see anybody there asking questions? A good-sized gent in a long duster?"

Bat shook his head and said, "Afraid not. Is that how he tracked you down?"

"Appears to be."

Sheriff Williamson said, "I'll go ask old Pete if anybody was nosing around his place earlier tonight."

"Better check at the other stable too," said Slocum.

"I will." The lawman looked hard at Slocum. "But first I want some straight answers from you."

"I've told you all I know," Slocum replied, his gaze equally flinty.

"The hell you have. There's more to this than you're lettin' on. Get your coat, Slocum. You're coming down to my office, and then you're goin' to spill whatever it is that's behind all this shootin' and killin'."

Slocum hesitated. He could get all muley and refuse to go with the sheriff, but that wouldn't accomplish anything in the long run. He nodded abruptly and said, "All right," and Williamson looked a little surprised at how easily Slocum had agreed to the demand. So did Bat and Billy, and for that matter Arabella.

He told Arabella that he would be back soon, then got the sheepskin jacket from her room and followed Williamson out of the place. Bat and Billy came along too, and the sheriff didn't bother pointing out that he hadn't invited them.

Slocum looked around as he and the other men walked down the street toward Williamson's office. A bitter cold wind was still blowing, but the light snow had stopped falling. The clouds overhead were breaking up again, and stars shone through the gaps. The street was deserted, which came as no surprise given the cold and the lateness of the hour.

A black, potbellied, cast-iron stove provided heat for Williamson's hole-in-the-wall office. A coffeepot was simmering on top of the stove, and Williamson poured cups of the thick black brew for all of them. The Arbuckle's was strong enough to sing and dance, as Slocum found when he took a sip—just the way he liked it.

Williamson sat down behind a scarred desk littered with papers and said, "Tell me about it, Slocum. The whole story."

Slocum did just that . . . sort of. He left out the part about killing the three buffalo hunters, sticking instead to the story he had told Mace Jones about finding the wagon and the mules on the prairie. He claimed he had found a woman and a baby out there too, and had made camp with them for one night. There was no point in telling the sheriff about how he and Rose had made love, so he skipped ahead to the next morning and his discovery that she had vanished, taking his horse with her. All in all, he estimated, what he told Williamson was about half of the truth, but that was enough for now.

Williamson seemed to believe him. "All right," the sheriff said with a grunt. "That still don't tell me who that fella was who took a shot at you and cut poor Jasper's throat."

Slocum could only shake his head. "I just don't know, Sheriff," he said. "I purely don't."

That statement, at least, was the whole truth and nothing but. Slocum had no idea who the gunman was or what his relationship to Rose and the baby might be.

But he figured that sooner or later, one way or another, he would find out. The stranger had wanted to find that baby badly enough to murder one man and threaten a woman with death. He wouldn't just let things go without making another try for Slocum.

And that was just what Slocum was counting on.

8

Sheriff Williamson promised that he would question Pete Sawyer and the owner of the other livery stable to find out if the gunman had paid them a visit. Slocum thought that was a foregone conclusion. The sheriff also planned to check every place in town where someone could rent a room. "Seems to me that if we can find the woman and the kid, we'll find out who that killer was," he said.

That was possible, Slocum conceded. There was definitely a connection between Rose and the gunman. Slocum hoped he found the man before Williamson did, though. He had a score to settle with the duster-clad stranger.

Bat and Billy both had rooms at the Deuces, so they walked with Slocum back to the saloon, flanking him again as they had before. Bat said, "The esteemed Sheriff Williamson seems to have the right of it, John. You do attract trouble."

Slocum grimaced. "Seems like hardly a month goes by that somebody's not shooting at me," he said. "But I don't set out looking for it—at least not most of the time."

Bat laughed and put a hand on his shoulder. "Don't worry. We'll keep you safe."

Easy enough to say, thought Slocum, *but where the hell were you when that gun-toting gent came busting into Arabella's room an hour ago?*

On the other hand, he mused, under the intimate circumstances just preceding that moment, he sure as blazes wouldn't have wanted Bat and Billy inside the room or even camped outside the door.

Arabella came to him as soon as he entered the saloon. "I had my talk with Sheriff Williamson," Slocum said, "but I don't think anything will come of it."

She regarded him solemnly. "It's time you told me what this is all about too, John. That is, if you know."

He shook his head and said, "Nary an inkling. But it's true, I *was* looking for a woman and a baby earlier today when I came into town. That seems to be what made that man come after me."

Arabella led him to a table while Bat and Billy stayed at the bar and signaled for Phil to bring them a couple of beers. Slocum and Arabella sat down, and Slocum told her the same story he had given the sheriff. Arabella nodded and said, "I know just about everyone in town. I'll spread the word that I want to know if anyone has seen such a woman with a child."

"Or even the woman by herself," Slocum said. "She could have the baby stashed somewhere."

Arabella nodded. "It would have to be somewhere warm and safe in weather like this." She stood up. "Give me until tomorrow, John. If the woman or the baby is in Tascosa, I'll know about it by then."

Slocum believed her. Saloonkeepers were usually some of the best-informed people in any frontier settlement. Surrounded by whiskey and women, most men seemed to get careless about any secrets they were trying to keep. If Rose was staying with someone in Tascosa, Arabella would probably be able to ferret out that fact.

And considering everything that had happened, Rose's mysterious disappearance had taken on more importance. Slocum had wanted to find her because he wanted to recover that lineback dun she had stolen. Now it looked like he might have to discover who she was and why she had that baby with her in order to save his own skin. If people kept trying to bushwhack him, sooner or later one of them might succeed.

He spent the night in one of the rooms down the hall from Arabella's quarters. If things had been different, he probably would have slept in that big bed of hers with her warm, naked body curled up beside him. But he didn't want to put her in danger again, so he thought it would be best to sleep alone.

Slocum slept hard, and didn't wake up until an hour or so after sunrise. He stayed where he was for a while, unwilling to crawl out from under the warm blankets piled on top of him. The mounting pressure in his bladder finally made him get up and hurriedly pull his clothes and boots on. It was cold enough in the room for his breath to fog in front of his face. A look out the single window showed him sunlight glittering on frost and snow. The sky was a deep, cloudless blue.

Slocum put on his hat and coat and went down the back stairs. Jasper's body had been removed, of course, and someone had tried to mop up the blood that had been spilled. The effort hadn't been completely successful; a dark, ugly stain had seeped into the floorboards and wouldn't come up. Slocum frowned at it as he went out. He had seen more death than most men and knew he had grown somewhat hardened to it, but cold-blooded murder still bothered him.

As he walked to the privy, he felt a light wind blowing from the south. The blue norther from two days earlier had played out. The south breeze and the sunshine would quickly warm things up. All the snow would be melted by the end of the day, Slocum knew, except that which had drifted into shady patches. That was Texas weather for you, he thought. By the next day, it might actually be hot again, then freezing cold and snowing again the day after that.

When he had relieved himself, he circled the saloon and stepped up onto the porch in front of the building. Tascosa appeared to be busier than it had been the day before. Wagons were parked in front of the stores, and several men on horseback moved along the street. Slocum's eyes rested on each rider in turn, making sure none of them was the man who had burst into Arabella's room.

That son of a bitch might be long gone, Slocum thought, but he doubted it. His instincts told him the gunman was still somewhere in the area.

The front door of the saloon opened, and Arabella said, "I thought I saw you out here, John. What on earth are you doing?"

"Just getting some fresh air," he told her.

"Well, come inside and have some breakfast."

Slocum accepted the invitation. The Deuces never really closed, but at this hour of the morning business was extremely light. Two men stood at the bar, being served by a single sleepy-eyed bartender. None of the percentage girls were in evidence. They were all upstairs asleep, Slocum supposed. The table where Arabella had been working on her ledger books the day before was now set for breakfast, and Bat Masterson was already sitting at one of the places. He grinned a greeting at Slocum.

"The rest of the night passed peacefully, I take it?"

Slocum nodded as he held Arabella's chair for her, then sat down himself. "That's right. Nobody else tried to kill me."

"That's always a good thing," said Bat. The plate in front of him was heaped with flapjacks, scrambled eggs, fried potatoes, and a thick, juicy steak. A smaller plate held biscuits with honey poured over them, and a steaming cup of coffee was at Bat's elbow. A similar meal was waiting for Arabella's attention, although the portions were considerably smaller.

An Asian man wearing a white cap and an apron over his clothes came out of a door behind the bar. He was carrying a plate filled with food, and he brought it over to the table and placed it in front of Slocum. He bowed deeply, revealing a long queue that hung down his back.

"Thank you, Wing," said Arabella.

"Need more, tell Wing," the cook said in a singsong voice. Hands steepled together in front of him, he bowed again and backed away from the table.

"Don't let that ignorant-coolie pose fool you," Arabella said when Wing had gone back through the door behind the bar into the kitchen. "He's an excellent cook and a very intelligent man."

Slocum couldn't speak to the second part of that statement, but a few bites of the breakfast placed before him confirmed the truth of the first part of Arabella's comment. The food was as good as Slocum had tasted since . . . well, since the night before, he reflected. Wing must have cooked the meal that Slocum and Arabella had shared in Arabella's quarters.

The food and a couple of cups of coffee cleared away any cobwebs left in Slocum's brain. By the time he pushed away his empty plate and leaned back in his chair, he felt a lot better—but he was no closer to making up his mind what he was going to do next.

As if she knew what he was thinking, Arabella sipped her own coffee and then asked, "What are your plans, John?"

Slocum shook his head. "I don't know."

"You could spend the winter here."

A world of meaning was packed into that simple statement, Slocum thought. He could spend the winter with her, that was what she meant. And he couldn't deny that it was an appealing prospect. Good food, plenty of whiskey, pleasant surroundings, a warm bed . . . and a lovely woman to share all of those things with him. He could pass the winter months quite easily here in Tascosa, and by playing poker while he was here, he could probably have quite a stake built up for himself by the time spring rolled around.

But in the years since the end of the war, he had hardly ever stayed that long in one place unless he was behind bars or laid up with an injury—and on those occasions he had almost gone mad. He was a drifter, plain and simple, and after a few days he couldn't wait to shake the dust of a place off his boots.

Besides, there was still the matter of Rose and Edgar, and the murdering son of a bitch who thought Slocum held the key to finding them.

To postpone any decision, he asked, "Have you had any luck finding out about that woman and the baby?"

Arabella shook her head. "None. I put the word out last night after you went to bed, but so far there's been no response."

"Billy and I talked to Pete Sawyer and that other stable man," Bat put in. "The sheriff had already been to see them, but they didn't mind telling us the same thing they told Cape." He leaned forward in his chair. "That hombre who broke in on you last night paid a visit to both stables. He asked about a woman and a baby at each place and got the same answer you did, John. Nobody has seen them. But Pete mentioned that you asked him about them, and so did the other fella. It seemed like an odd coincidence to both of them, and neither of them saw any harm in saying something about it."

"I didn't warn them to keep it to themselves," Slocum said. "Reckon that was my mistake."

"I described the man to Phil as best I could," said Arabella, "and after he thought about it, he decided that the man was in here a short while before the trouble began. He had one drink and then left, and no one thought anything about it. But obviously, he asked enough questions while he was here to discover that you had gone upstairs." She blushed. "With me."

"Then he went around back, killed Jasper, and came up the stairs," Slocum finished. He nodded slowly. The bits and pieces of the puzzle fit together, all right, but they didn't form a picture. Not yet anyway.

Bat regarded Slocum thoughtfully and said, "I think I know what's going on in that head of yours, John. You're going to keep looking for the woman."

"She's out there somewhere," Slocum said stubbornly, "and she's what this is all about. Either her or that baby, or both."

"You can wait a while and let me see if I can find out anything," Arabella said. "Another day or two perhaps."

Slocum considered. Every hour he waited, the trail grew that much colder. On the other hand, if he left Tascosa and Rose was really hidden out somewhere here in the settlement, he'd be riding away from the answers he wanted.

"I'll give it until this afternoon," he decided. "If you're going to hear anything, Arabella, it should have been by then. If not, I'll see about getting a horse and hit the trail to the south. She wouldn't have gone back into the teeth of that storm, so she must've headed in that direction." He looked at Bat. "You and Billy want to ride along?"

Regretfully, Bat shook his head. "I'm sorry, John. I think I can speak for Billy when I say we'd like to. But now that the weather has cleared, we're off for Dodge City. We've been planning to go for weeks now, and I don't want to miss another opportunity."

Slocum grinned. "Sounds to me like there's a pretty woman in Dodge you plan on visiting."

"Not at all," Bat replied easily. "My brother Jim owns a dance hall there, and good old Ed, the eldest of the Masterson boys, has become a lawman. I was thinking of following in the footsteps of one of them."

Slocum could easily imagine Bat running a dance hall or a saloon, but despite the comments Bat had made to Sheriff Williamson the day before, Slocum just couldn't see him packing a badge. Whatever he did, though, he would probably be a success at it—unless somebody shot him first.

"Well, good luck to you," Slocum said. "Have a drink with me before you go."

"We'll do that," Bat promised.

Slocum spent the morning sitting with Arabella and talking about nothing in a companionable way. From time to time as he looked across the table at her, he felt a pang of regret that he had decided to ride on. But he had never been able to leave things unfinished, and he had a hunch this business with Rose would come back to haunt him if he turned his back on it.

Bat Masterson and Billy Dixon came by the Deuces just before midday and had that farewell drink with Slocum. He shook hands with both of them and said, "If I get up Dodge City way next spring, I'll look you up."

"I probably won't be there," Billy said. "There are still

enough buffalo down here in the Panhandle to make things interesting for a little while yet. But Bat'll be around in Dodge, I reckon. He's about ready to settle down, maybe go to work clerking in a dry-goods store.''

''That'll be the day,'' Bat said with a laugh.

They downed the rest of their beers and left the saloon with a friendly wave. Slocum was sorry to see them go, but he didn't brood about it. That was the way things were out here on the frontier. Folks came into your life for a while, and sometimes what they did was good and sometimes bad, but either way they moved on and a man was alone. Slocum was used to it.

His own deadline for leaving was coming up. He pulled his watch from his pocket, flipped it open, and checked the time. Nearly noon. He ought to mosey down to the livery stable and talk to Pete Sawyer about a horse, he supposed.

Arabella put a soft hand on his arm. ''I know what you're thinking, John,'' she said quietly. ''Before you go . . . come upstairs with me.''

The smart thing to do would be to turn down the offer, Slocum thought. But he couldn't bring himself to do it. The longing in Arabella's eyes was too plain to see, and he wanted her as badly as she wanted him.

They didn't make any pretense of going upstairs separately. As soon as the door of her room was closed behind them, she turned and reached out to him, and Slocum took her into his arms. There was an unspoken urgency in the kiss and in the way they clutched each other. What passed between them now would have to last them both through what might be a long, cold winter.

Slocum stripped her clothes away as she pulled his off. A small fire had been left burning in the fireplace, and combined with the increasing warmth of the day outside, it made the room almost hot. Slocum ran his hands over her body, his caresses rough and impatient. As he cupped her breasts and strummed the erect nipples with his thumbs, she closed her eyes, tipped her head back, and moaned at the intensity of the sensations running through her. Slocum felt pretty intense himself as she dropped her hands to his groin, closing one of them around his shaft and using the other to cradle the sac beneath it.

She lifted her mouth to his and slid her tongue between his lips. The urgency they both felt grew even greater. When she pulled back he went with her, and they sprawled across the silk coverlet on the bed.

Arabella's knees lifted and her legs parted, and Slocum moved between them, ready to enter her with one thrust of his hips. She stopped him, though, placing her hands on his chest and saying, "Wait." Slocum was in no mood to delay, but he let Arabella have her way. She rolled him over onto his back and then straddled him, placing a knee on each side of his hips. The long, thick pole of his manhood was aimed straight up at her. She rested her hands on his chest again and slowly lowered herself onto it, sheathing it with the hot, wet core of her femininity.

Breathing heavily, Arabella raised her torso until she was sitting upright on him, his shaft buried deeply within her. Her inner muscles clasped him tightly, and she gasped as his manhood throbbed and swelled even more in response. "You fill me up, John," she said in a voice made husky by passion. "You fill me up so wonderfully. There's been no one like you since . . . since forever."

Slocum lifted his hips, driving into her. She began to pump back and forth on top of him, moving faster and faster, her breath rasping in her throat. She reached behind her and braced her hands on his thighs so that she could put more force into her movements. Slocum reached up and caught hold of her bobbing breasts, cupping and kneading them.

He saw the flush of her climax spreading across her throat and the upper slopes of her breasts. Her eyes were closed again and her lips were parted. She gave a sharp exhalation of breath every time he pistoned home inside her. Lovemaking so intense couldn't last very long, and it didn't. Slocum slid his hands off her breasts and dropped them to her hips, holding her still as he plunged to the utmost depth one final time. He shuddered as he pumped his seed into her.

Arabella fell forward onto his chest. She nuzzled against him, kissing his throat and then lifting her mouth to his once more. Slocum put his arms around her and returned the kiss. The urgency they had both felt earlier had fled, and now there was only tenderness. God, Slocum was going to miss her!

Someone knocked on the door.

Arabella's head jerked up, and Slocum's hand shot out to the butt of the Colt, which he had carefully placed on a chair even closer to the bed this time. "Damn it!" he grated. "What is it now?"

"At least no one has kicked the door in," Arabella said wryly. His shaft was still buried inside her, and her breasts were flattened against his chest. She turned her head toward the door and called, "Who is it?"

"It's, uh, me, Miss Arabella." Slocum recognized Phil's voice as the hesitant reply came back. The bartender sounded mighty embarrassed—as well he should be.

"What do you want?" Arabella asked.

"Well, I, uh . . . I hate to disturb you, but there's this young fella downstairs . . . he's mighty upset, and he's looking for Mr. Slocum."

Arabella looked at Slocum. They were equally surprised and puzzled. If the killer from the night before had shown up, Phil wouldn't have meekly come up here and knocked on the door. He would have signaled the bouncers to jump the man instead. This had to be someone else.

"What does he want?" called Arabella.

Phil's answer came back through the door. "Like I said, he's really upset . . . and he claims he wants to hire Mr. Slocum to help him find his wife and his baby."

9

Babies again! Slocum gritted his teeth and sat up, his softening manhood slipping out of Arabella as he did so. He felt a pang of regret and loss, and judging by the expression on her face, so did she. But Slocum had to find out what was going on, so he reached for his pants as he called, "I'll be downstairs in a minute, Phil."

Arabella put a hand on his arm. "Be careful, John," she said softly.

Slocum shook his head. "Whoever this is looking for me, he's not going to try anything in broad daylight, in the middle of the biggest saloon in town. Maybe he's got some of the answers I've been looking for."

He shrugged into his shirt and vest, then sat down on the edge of the bed to pull on his socks and boots.

Arabella had stood up and was wrapping a silk robe around her, covering up all that firm, warm, creamy flesh. Slocum sighed at the thought of it.

All that was left was buckling on his gunbelt. He did so, then checked the Colt Navy to make sure it slipped easily from the cross-draw holster. He didn't think he'd need it, but it never hurt to be careful.

Phil had gone back downstairs. As Slocum started down the staircase, he caught the eye of the bartender, who was back behind the hardwood. Phil nodded toward a slender young man sitting at one of the tables. The Deuces was busier than it had been earlier in the day; a dozen men were standing at the bar, and several of the tables were occupied, including the one that was Slocum's destination. A poker game was already going on at one of the other tables.

The young man had his hands wrapped around a whiskey glass, cradling it carefully as he lifted it toward his lips. His hands were trembling slightly, Slocum noted. He wore a town suit that might have been expensive once but had seen a lot of hard wear since then, and perched on his fair hair was a derby that was battered and scuffed. Several days' worth of beard stubble dotted his cheeks, but it was hard to see because it was so light in color. Slocum couldn't tell if he was armed or not.

Slocum came to a stop beside the table. "I'm John Slocum," he said. "I hear you're looking for me."

The young man tossed off the rest of the drink in his glass and then set it on the table with equal caution. He swallowed and looked up. "S-sit down," he said through gritted teeth. When he relaxed slightly, his teeth began to chatter. He was chilled to the bone, Slocum realized. He needed a tub of warm water and a few more drinks of whiskey to thaw him out.

Slocum used his left hand to pull out a chair. He sat down and asked bluntly, "Who are you?"

"M-my name is . . . Calvin D-Delaney," the young man forced out. "I think you know my . . . w-wife."

Slocum drew a deep breath. "You're married to Rose?"

"Y-yes. Edgar is our s-son."

Slocum frowned. He was sitting across the table from a man he had cuckolded two nights earlier. This wasn't the first time he had run across the husband of a woman who had shared his bed—or in this case, his blankets—but it was still a disconcerting experience. Slocum didn't feel guilty. He'd had no way of knowing that Rose was married, and if she had wanted him to know, she should have told him. But he felt a little uncomfortable anyway as he looked at Calvin Delaney.

"How do you know I have anything to do with your wife and child?" asked Slocum.

The warmth of the saloon seemed to be helping Delaney a little, and the fire lit in his belly by that whiskey probably helped too. His voice was a bit stronger as he said, "I asked around town and was told that you had been looking for them. You met them out on the prairie, or something like that?"

"That's right," Slocum admitted. "They were caught out in that blue norther that came through a couple of days ago. I was going to bring them into town here, but your wife had other ideas. She took off on her own." A harder edge crept into his voice. "She took my horse with her when she left."

"I'm sorry, Mr. Slocum, I truly am. Rose is . . . is impulsive sometimes."

That explained why she had seduced him so brazenly. She'd had an itch, and she had scratched it. But it didn't answer the more important questions.

"What was she doing out there alone on the plains with that baby?"

Delaney's eyes were downcast as he answered, "That was my fault, I suppose. We'd had an argument. . . . You see, we were on our way to Santa Fe, and Rose got angry with me and rode off with Edgar. I . . . I knew from past experience that she would get over it and come back to me when she cooled off, so I didn't go after her." Delaney's face contorted in grief and self-recrimination. "God, why didn't I go after her and beg her to forgive me?" he choked out. "I could have stopped her, brought her back to the wagon. . . ."

"But you didn't, and when she didn't come back, you got worried."

"I didn't know where she could be! I tried to look for her, but I . . . I don't know this country."

Slocum had already guessed that from his accent. "Where are you from?"

"St. Louis. But like I said, we were moving to Santa Fe."

"You loaded your family in a wagon and started out from St. Louis to Santa Fe at this time of year?"

Delaney nodded. "I felt like we . . . we needed to make a new start."

"You're a damned fool," snapped Slocum, "and you've maybe gotten your wife and baby killed because of it."

For a second, anger flashed in Calvin Delaney's eyes. Slocum expected the young man to tell him that he had no right to talk to him that way. But then the anger faded and Delaney nodded meekly. "You're right, Mr. Slocum," he said. "You're my only hope now."

Slocum sighed in exasperation. "I've already been looking for your wife, and I haven't found her. What makes you think I can?"

"A man like you, a true Westerner, you'd stand a lot better chance than I ever would. I can pay you—"

"How long ago was it your wife ran off from you?" Slocum cut in.

"It was . . . two days ago. Early that morning."

The same day he had found Rose, thought Slocum, the day of the blue norther. So she and Edgar hadn't been out on their own for very long when they encountered the buffalo hunters, and it hadn't been long after that when Slocum came along to rescue them. If he had known then that Calvin Delaney was so close, he probably could have reunited the family. . . .

But even after her terrifying experience with Green and Harper and Keever, Rose hadn't wanted to go back to her husband. She was so determined not to return to Calvin that she had even lied to Slocum about Edgar being her child. Slocum had suspected that was the case. Rose must've really been mad at her husband, he mused. Maybe she had good reason. Something about Calvin Delaney rubbed him the wrong way.

And nothing Delaney had told him explained who the big man in the duster was, or why *he* was searching for Rose and Edgar.

"You were traveling alone, no guides or anybody else riding with you?"

Delaney shook his head. "There was just the three of us. And now there . . . there's just me." His face twisted again, and for a second Slocum thought he was going to start crying. Slocum grimaced in disgust.

"You said you looked for her?"

Delaney swallowed and said, "I . . . I drove through that storm until I thought I was going to freeze to death. I still can't get warmed up." A shudder went through him. "But there was never any sign of her. I . . . I found this town pretty much by accident, and when I got here I started asking questions right away . . . and that led me to you."

Slocum nodded. The man in the duster could have been somebody else Rose ran into after disappearing from the camp they had made. Slocum didn't know who else he could have been. That didn't explain why the man had been willing to kill in order to find Rose and the baby—but maybe Rose could answer that question.

"I'm going to keep looking for your wife," Slocum told Calvin Delaney. "I planned to ride out and head south pretty soon. You can come along if you want, but you'll have to keep up with me."

"I can do that," said Delaney, but he didn't sound too convinced of it. The words had the hollow sound of an empty boast. "And like I said, I can pay you—"

"You can buy some supplies. That'll be enough for now." Slocum generally wasn't overly particular about how and where he got his cash, but he didn't want any of this pathetic pilgrim's money. He didn't want to feel like he owed anything to Calvin Delaney.

Delaney nodded. "All right. I have a wagon."

"So do I, but I won't be taking it. We'll need saddle horses." Slocum scraped his chair back. "Come on down to the livery stable. We'll see what we can work out."

"Thank you, Mr. Slocum," Delaney said as he got to his feet. "I can't tell you how much this means to me."

"Then don't try." Slocum went to get his Stetson and his sheepskin jacket. The thought of hitting the trail with Delaney wasn't very appealing, but he couldn't deny the man the opportunity to help look for his wife and child.

He left the Deuces with Delaney tagging along behind him.

•   •   •

Pete Sawyer proved to be as shrewd a horse trader as Slocum
had thought he would be. The old stable keeper was willing
to take in both wagons, the mule team that had belonged to
the buffalo hunters, and the oxen that Delaney had been using
to pull his wagon. In return he offered two saddle horses, two
packhorses, and a pair of saddles. The saddle horses weren't
bad mounts, Slocum judged, but the pack animals were plugs
and nearly worthless.

"I want better packhorses," Slocum said, "so that we can
switch back and forth and make better time."

Sawyer rubbed his grizzled jaw and squinted in thought. "I
don't know that I can do any better," he said slowly. "This
is getting to be cow country. Not much call for wagons. And
hosses are worth more than mules or oxen."

"You can sell those wagons to some of the buffalo hunters
next spring, and you know it," Slocum pointed out.

"That's in the spring. What do I do 'tween now and then,
whilst those wagons are just sittin' and gatherin' dust?"

Slocum didn't answer. Instead he walked along the broad center aisle of the livery barn to the back doors, which stood open.
The horses had been taken out of their stalls and hazed into the
corral to get some sun and fresh air. They cropped lazily at the
few patches of grass that were left. Slocum studied them for a
moment, then pointed to a black gelding and a roan mare. "I'll
take those two for pack animals and spare mounts." The black
and the roan weren't exceptional animals, but at least they
weren't as broken down as the two Sawyer had originally offered.

The liveryman frowned. "Them are fine hosses," he observed.

"There's another stable in town," said Slocum.

Sawyer sighed. "All right. You drive a hard bargain, Slocum, but I reckon I can see my way clear to goin' along with
you. You don't want to do business with that other fella. He'll
cheat you, sure as the day is long."

Slocum had a feeling the other stable owner would have

said exactly the same thing about Sawyer. He didn't care one way or the other about their rivalry; all he wanted was some horses he could depend on.

Calvin Delaney had watched the negotiations in silence. As Slocum and Sawyer turned away from the corral, Sawyer jerked a thumb at him and asked, ''Who's that?''

''Just a fella who's going to be riding with me.''

Sawyer snorted. ''Looks like a no-account to me.''

Slocum shrugged and didn't say anything. Privately, he shared Sawyer's opinion of Delaney, but if he was going to be traveling with the man, it didn't make sense to treat him with open contempt. Slocum's comments in the saloon had been sharp enough, and he would leave it at that.

''We'll be back to pick up the horses in half an hour,'' Slocum told Sawyer. ''Come on, Delaney.''

The two of them paid a visit next to one of Tascosa's general stores. Slocum had the proprietor gather up an order of supplies, mostly staples such as flour, sugar, coffee, beans, and bacon. He turned to Delaney and asked, ''Have you got a gun?''

''A Henry rifle and a Smith & Wesson pistol.''

''Can you use them?''

''I can shoot a little,'' Delaney said. His voice was tentative, and Slocum wouldn't have wanted to place much confidence in him if it came down to a fight. He had the store owner add some ammunition for both weapons to the order, along with more cartridges for his Winchester. When the bill was totaled up, Slocum paid part of it, and Delaney made up the difference. Slocum nodded in satisfaction as he hefted the saddlebags in which the supplies had been packed.

''Let's get back down to the livery and pick up those horses.''

He was making no secret of the fact that he was leaving town. If that duster-clad gunman wanted to follow them, he would have no trouble doing it. Slocum figured they didn't need to be afraid of an ambush, at least not from that source. The gunman wanted to know where Rose was. Maybe he would be content to hang back and follow them for a while, waiting to see if they found Rose before he made his move.

If that was the way the hand played out, Slocum intended to be ready for him.

Nor had Slocum forgotten about Mace Jones and the other buffalo hunters. That situation was a little more worrisome. Mace might be willing to take another long-distance potshot at him. But Slocum wasn't going to just lie low all winter. He had things to do.

He should have killed Mace during that first confrontation, he told himself. He should have drawn and fired as soon as Bat Masterson and Billy Dixon rode up. It never paid for a man to leave an enemy alive behind him.

But it was too late now, so he would just have to rely on his instincts and the survival skills developed over long years on the frontier to keep him alive until he found Rose Delaney. As for her husband . . . well, Calvin Delaney would have to take his own chances. Slocum would keep him alive if possible, but he wouldn't risk his own life for the man.

Pete Sawyer had saddled the two horses Slocum had chosen as the primary mounts, an Appaloosa and a gray. Slocum fastened the saddlebags in place on the pack animals, then took the Appaloosa's reins. "Take the gray," he said to Delaney. "I want to stop by the Deuces before we leave." He planned to check with Arabella one last time and make sure she hadn't had any word about Rose from the feelers she had put out.

And truth to tell, he wanted to say a proper good-bye too. There was no way of knowing when he would make it back to Tascosa, if ever, or if Arabella would still be here when he did.

He led the Appaloosa and the packhorses down the street to the saloon. Delaney managed to awkwardly lead the gray. They tied the animals to the hitch rack outside the saloon and stepped up onto the porch. Slocum opened the door, feeling a pang of nostalgia for the place already—and he wasn't even gone yet.

Arabella stood at the bar. Her face was carefully expressionless as Slocum came over to her. He could tell she was making an effort not to break down and beg him to stay. For a plugged nickel, he almost would have done it.

His eyes locked with hers, and despite the fact that the saloon was getting crowded, for a moment it was like they were the only two people in the room. "I'll be riding on now," Slocum said quietly, and Arabella gave him a calm, composed nod.

"I know. I'm sorry, John, but I haven't heard anything about that woman or the baby. I don't think they ever came to Tascosa."

"Looks like you're probably right. She must have gone around the settlement and headed on south. I intend to find her." Slocum glanced over his shoulder at Delaney. "This fella is her husband. He's going to be riding with me."

Arabella gave Delaney a distracted smile. "I hope you find your wife, sir. My prayers will be with you."

Delaney tugged on the brim of his derby and said, "Thank you, ma'am."

Arabella turned back to Slocum. "Will you ever ride this way again, John?"

"I imagine so. I drift around so much that you never know where I'll pop up next." He managed to grin a little as he spoke.

She leaned toward him. "Come back," she whispered. "Remember me . . . and come back." Her lips pressed warmly to his for a moment.

"I'm not likely to forget," Slocum said, his voice hoarse with emotion. He had known Arabella less than twenty-four hours, but a bond had sprung up immediately between them, and had only grown stronger during the time they had spent together. He reached up, put a hand behind her neck, and held her as he kissed her, harder this time.

Then he let go of her, turned away, and strode toward the door without looking back. He assumed that Calvin Delaney was following him, but at the moment he didn't really give a damn one way or the other.

You're the biggest fool in the world, John Slocum, he told himself. *You could stay here with that woman.*

But if he did, the questions that were gnawing at him would go unanswered, and Slocum knew he couldn't live with that. For his own peace of mind, he had to put Tascosa behind him as soon as possible.

10

The warmer weather held, and no one tried to kill them. Those were about the only good things Slocum could say about the next couple of days.

He and Delaney followed the Canadian River, which trended southeast, for a ways before turning almost due south on an old but well-defined Indian trail. This would take them to Palo Duro Canyon and Charley Goodnight's ranch. Slocum planned to stop there and ask Goodnight if Rose had turned up at the ranch. Slocum had ridden for a spell with Goodnight's cowboys while the cattle baron and his partner, Oliver Loving, had been moving hundred of thousands of cattle over the trail they had established to New Mexico Territory and Colorado. He thought Goodnight might remember him.

Calvin Delaney kept up, as Slocum had warned him he would have to, matching the pace Slocum set without much trouble. However, the weather was good and the going was pretty easy. Slocum didn't know how Delaney would do when things got tougher, as they inevitably would.

A couple of days after leaving Tascosa, Delaney was riding alongside Slocum when he lifted his arm and pointed to a low, dark smudge in the distance. "What's that?" he asked.

Slocum was rocking easily in the saddle. He peered off in the direction Delaney indicated and said after a moment,

"Buffalo. About half a million of them, I'd guess."

Delaney's eyes widened. "Half a million buffalo?" he repeated.

Slocum nodded. "Yep. It's a small bunch."

"They look like . . . like an ocean of brown hides."

"You're just about right." Slocum still didn't like Delaney; that was instinctive, and there was nothing he could do about it. But he wasn't above reminiscing a little, even in company such as this. He stretched his back, easing tired muscles, and went on. "I camped on a ridge once overlooking a valley so wide I couldn't see the other side of it. That valley was filled as far as the eye could see from east to west and north to south with buffalo. They were migrating, so they kept moving steady. They never stopped for the whole three days I was camped there, and they were still going by when I gave up and turned around and went back the way I'd come. I figure more than a million went by every day I was there."

"That's incredible. I'd heard about the vast numbers of the beasts out here on the frontier, but I never dreamed . . . never really understood just how many there really are."

"Were," said Slocum. "They've been killed off by the hundreds of thousands. The big herds used to be up in Kansas and Nebraska. Now most of the ones that are left have moved down here to the Panhandle. They keep drifting south, and the hunters keep killing them as they go. There'll come a time when there aren't any left."

"Does that bother you?"

"Don't know why it should," Slocum said. "Buffalo don't mean anything to me."

But that wasn't entirely true, he thought bleakly. The buffalo wasn't the only breed that was dying off.

The plains scenery was monotonous. Slocum and Delaney rode and camped, rode and camped. Slocum kept a close eye out for horse tracks, hoping to find Rose's trail. The only tracks they found, though, were those of unshod Indian ponies. Those trails all led east, toward the reservations in Indian Territory. The Comanches were going in for the winter, content to let the white men feed them until spring came again. Then, a few might head back out to the prairie to raid and hunt as they had done in the old days—some four or five years earlier. The others, seduced by reservation life even though in many ways it was a hellish existence, would remain in Indian Territory.

Slocum watched their back trail closely too, but if anyone was following them, they were doing a good job of it. He didn't spot anyone.

They were four days out of Tascosa and looking for a place to camp in the late afternoon. Slocum saw a grassy hill rising to the east. That wouldn't be a bad spot to spend the night, he decided. The hill's elevation would give them a commanding view of the countryside for miles around. But it would have to be a cold camp, because lighting a fire on top of that hill would have been like a beacon, attracting anyone who was looking for trouble.

Slocum was riding the Appaloosa, Delaney the roan. As he veered his mount toward the hill, Slocum said, "We'll make camp up there."

Delaney followed without comment. So far, he hadn't challenged any of Slocum's decisions. He seemed to know just what a tenderfoot he was and how lucky he was to be alive after being caught out in that blue norther.

They had just started up the slope when a red ray from the lowering sun glinted garishly off something at the top of the hill.

Slocum pitched out of his saddle without thinking, and while he was in midair he heard the flat *whap!* of a heavy-caliber bullet passing through the space he had just occupied. The dull boom of the rifle came an instant later, as Slocum was slamming into the ground and rolling over. He gasped because the impact had knocked some of the air out of his lungs. It was a second before he could yell at Delaney, "Get down! Get down!"

Delaney had already gotten the idea. He let out a frightened shout as he jerked his horse to the side, away from Slocum.

He may not have meant to, but as the roan danced skittishly, spooked by the sudden action, Delaney slipped from the saddle and toppled to the ground. The derby went flying as he fell. He landed hard on his back and didn't move.

Another slug whipped by as Slocum scrambled to his feet and lunged toward the Appaloosa. The horse shied away from him, but Slocum's outstretched fingers closed around the reins and jerked the animal to a stop. Slocum ducked behind the Appaloosa, using its body to shield him from the bushwhacker on top of the hill as he reached over the saddle and grasped the butt of the Winchester sticking up from the saddle boot.

He yanked the rifle free just as the Appaloosa reared up and pulled the reins from Slocum's hand. An ugly thud sounded, and the horse let out a shrill whinny of pain. It toppled toward Slocum, blood welling from the bullet hole in its neck where one of the bushwhacker's shots had struck it.

Slocum leaped back from the dying horse. He had no idea what was happening to Calvin Delaney, but there was no time to check on the man. The Appaloosa crashed to the ground, its legs kicking spasmodically for a few seconds before the stillness of death settled over the corpse. Slocum sprawled behind the dead horse, using it for cover as he lined his Winchester on the top of the hill and started firing.

The angle was bad. Slocum had always hated shooting uphill like this. What made it worse was that the horse's body didn't completely shelter him from the fire of the bushwhackers, but he drew his legs up and made himself into as small a target as possible. There was more than one man up there, he had decided. From the sound of the shots, they were coming from buffalo rifles, and they were too close together to be one man.

Mace Jones and his friends, thought Slocum. Had to be.

He emptied the Winchester, raking the hilltop with his fire, then ducked his head down behind the dead horse and reached into the pocket of his jacket for the box of shells he carried there. As he began reloading the Winchester, he hoped that the duster-clad gunman from Tascosa really *was* somewhere in the area, trailing him and Delaney. The man wanted Slocum alive, so if he was nearby, maybe he would take a hand in this fight.

Through long years of practice, Slocum was able to reload the rifle by feel, so he turned his head and looked for Calvin Delaney. The man was lying facedown about twenty yards away, behind a little hummock of dirt with some dead grass sticking out the top of it. He wasn't moving. Slocum called softly, "Delaney! You hit? Delaney!"

Delaney turned his head so that Slocum could see his face, proving that he was still alive anyway. His features were pale with terror, washed completely free of color. "Oh, God!" he cried. "What's going on, Mr. Slocum?"

"Somebody's trying to kill us," Slocum answered—somewhat unnecessarily, he thought. Even somebody from St. Louis should have known what was happening here. "Are you hurt?"

"I . . . I don't think so. When I fell, it knocked all the breath out of me. A bullet hit so close to me that the dust it kicked up got in my eyes, but then I was able to roll over and crawl over here."

Delaney's good luck was still with him. By all rights, Mace and the other buffalo hunters should have riddled him with bullets while he was lying out in the open. But even though shooting downhill was easier than firing uphill, it still made for some tricky shots. Delaney had just been fortunate.

That good luck likely wouldn't last. Slocum knew they were pinned down. If Mace and the others had plenty of ammunition, they could sit up there for hours and keep plunking away at him and Delaney.

On the other hand, the sun was setting, and it would be dark in less than an hour. The moon wouldn't rise for a while, meaning Slocum and Delaney would have a chance to sneak away in the thick darkness—if they lived that long.

Mace didn't intend to take that chance. The sound of hoofbeats came to Slocum's ears, followed a second later by loud, raucous whoops. Slocum lifted his head.

Mace and his friends were charging.

Mace knew as well as Slocum that the ambush had come too late in the day. The buffalo hunters had followed them from Tascosa, more than likely pushed on around them during one of the nights, then found this spot and set up their ambush. But the timing of Slocum's arrival hadn't cooperated with their plans, so now that Slocum and Delaney were unhorsed, Mace and the others were going to try to overrun them and finish them off. They stood a good chance of doing just that, thundering down the hillside as they were, shouting and firing their six-guns as they came.

Slocum lurched to his knees, lifting the Winchester. He saw the long buffalo-hide coats of the hunters flapping behind them as they galloped toward him. The butt of the rifle socked into his shoulder as he lined the sights on Mace's broad chest. But just as Slocum squeezed the trigger, Mace let out a Comanche-like yip and veered his mount abruptly to Slocum's left. Slocum's shot whined past him harmlessly.

There were four hunters in the group, counting Mace. They split up, as if according to a prearranged plan, two going to the right, the other two to the left. Slocum bit back a curse. He couldn't fire in two directions at once, and he would be lucky to be able to down more than one of the men. Within a matter of seconds, the hunters were going to have him in a cross fire, and that would be the end of this fight.

"Delaney!" yelled Slocum. "Get those two on your side!"

That was a real longshot, hoping that Delaney could even pull his Smith & Wesson and get off a round, let alone hit anything. But to Slocum's surprise, the pistol began cracking wickedly.

He couldn't turn to see what results Delaney was having. The other hunter on his side cut in front of Mace, so Slocum settled for drawing a bead on him. A slug whined by Slocum's ear, uncomfortably close, just as he fired.

The bullet took the buffalo hunter in the chest and lifted him from the saddle, spinning him around in the air. Over the thunder of hoofbeats, Slocum heard the man's choked cry of surprised agony. Slocum worked the Winchester's lever. Mace was almost on top of him now. Slocum twisted, throwing himself backward against the dead horse. His legs were stretched out in front of him and he was lying almost flat on his back as Mace swept by. A bullet slammed into the ground next to Slocum's head, and another thudded into the Appaloosa's body. Slocum's lips pulled back from his teeth in a grimace of hate as he jerked the Winchester's trigger and worked the lever, firing again and again as fast as he could.

To his amazement, he saw the pistol go flying from Mace's hand. One of the rifle bullets must have hit the big hunter's arm, Slocum thought. Mace was hit even harder than that, he realized after a second. He saw Mace grab the horn and slump in the saddle, almost falling from the horse. The horse kept running, and Mace seemed to be holding on for dear life.

Satisfied that Mace was no longer an immediate threat, Slocum rolled over and looked toward the hummock where Calvin Delaney had been lying. Delaney was still there, but he was up on his knees in a crouch, the Smith & Wesson gripped tightly in both hands and extended out in front of him. He was no longer firing the pistol, which was probably empty, judging by the way he had been snapping off shots earlier. What Slocum saw when he looked past Delaney astonished him even more than the sight of Mace dropping his pistol.

Both of the other buffalo hunters were sprawled motionless on the ground. Their horses had run off about fifty yards and then stopped to crop listlessly at the brown grass.

Slocum glanced toward Mace again and saw that the hunter was still on his horse, pounding on toward the west and growing smaller by the moment. He showed no signs of turning around and continuing the fight. Hell, thought Slocum, Mace might already be unconscious or even dead, held in the saddle by the death-grip he had locked on the horn.

"Delaney!" Slocum snapped as he turned back toward the pilgrim. "Are you all right?"

"I . . . I think so." Delaney's voice shook a little as he answered.

Slocum looked down at his own left arm as a stinging pain started. The sleeve of the sheepskin jacket was ripped, as was the sleeve of the shirt under it. Through the torn garments, Slocum glimpsed blood welling slowly from a shallow groove on his arm. One of Mace's bullets had grazed him, and he hadn't even been aware of it at the time.

"Better check yourself over," Slocum advised Delaney. "Sometimes you're hit and you don't even know it."

"I'm all right," Delaney insisted, his voice a little stronger now. He got to his feet and took a lurching step toward the men lying on the prairie.

Slocum stood and moved quickly to Delaney's side. There were still a few rounds left in the Winchester's magazine, should either of the fallen buffalo hunters prove to still be alive and dangerous. "Stay back," Slocum said. He went past Delaney and checked both bodies, rolling them onto their backs with a booted foot. The two buffalo hunters were dead, both of them struck in the head by bullets from Delaney's gun.

Slocum glanced at Delaney through eyes narrowed by suspicion, then took long strides back to the third hunter, the one he had shot out of the saddle. That man was dead too, just as Slocum had thought. Slocum lowered the rifle and relaxed a little as he turned back toward Delaney.

Delaney still held the Smith & Wesson, but now it was lying loosely in the palm of his hand while he stared down at it as if he had never even seen a gun before. He looked up at Slocum and said, "How . . . how . . ."

"Reckon you must be a better shot than I thought you were," Slocum said dryly. "Either that, or you're the luckiest son of a bitch I've ever run across, Delaney."

"They . . . they were right on top of me," Delaney said after swallowing hard. "I didn't have any choice . . . I just stuck the gun up and started shooting. . . ."

"You did just fine," said Slocum, thinking that he had never expected to be saying those words to Delaney.

"Why did these men attack us?" Delaney asked as he looked around at the bodies.

Before answering, Slocum looked around and tried to locate Mace again. But Mace and his horse had vanished into the distance. Slocum didn't think the buffalo hunter would be back.

"It's a long story," Slocum said in answer to Delaney's question. "Let's round up our horses, catch the ones that those bastards were riding, and make camp up there like we planned to. Then I'll tell you all about it."

11

Mace Jones fought onward against the sea of pain that threatened to engulf him. One of Slocum's bullets had drilled through his right forearm, taking a chunk of meat with it but luckily missing the bone. Another slug had ventilated the thick buffalo coat and ripped a shallow gash in Mace's left side. The wound was painful and had made him bleed like a stuck pig for a while, and losing all that blood had made him weak and light-headed. Still, he would have turned back and faced down Slocum and that sharpshooting, pasty-faced son of a bitch—whoever *he* was—if not for the fact that he had seen his three companions go down. Alone and wounded against Slocum and the other man, he would have just gotten himself killed, and Mace knew it.

Better to wait, try to heal up, and bide his time until he could strike again at the man he had vowed to kill.

Not that he'd been particularly close to Green and Harper and Keever, Mace realized as he rode slowly, each step of the horse making fresh waves of pain go through him. Truth to tell, the trio of buffalo hunters who had been killed by Slocum before he stole their outfit were about as sorry-ass a bunch as Mace had ever known. Any one of them would have cut his own mother's throat for a five-dollar gold piece, and the degenerate sons o' bitches would hump just about anything female, no matter how young or old or ugly. No, Mace didn't miss them, not one bit.

But they'd been buffalo hunters, damn it, like him, and he had to avenge their murders. A fella had to stick together with folks in the same line of work, whether he liked them or not.

Those thoughts and others less coherent whirled around and around inside Mace's head as he rode. He started cursing the man called Slocum, the oaths coming from him in a slurred, strained voice that grew louder and louder. Mace got so carried away in his tirade of profanity that he didn't even notice when his grip on the saddlehorn slipped and he started to fall.

He felt it when he crashed into the ground, though. Agony rippled through him, radiating outward from the wound in his side and, to a lesser extent, from the bullet hole in his arm. He whimpered and gasped for breath, his fingers clawing spasmodically at the ground, as the pain gradually receded slightly. He rolled onto his back and gazed up at a bright silver light in the sky. It was the moon, he realized after a moment. Night had fallen hours earlier without him taking note of it.

Something moved between Mace and the moon, blocking the silvery illumination. Mace stiffened as his bleary eyes finally locked on the tall, broad-shouldered figure looming over him.

"Slocum?" he croaked. "That you, Slocum? Come to finish me off, have you, you son of a bitch? Well, do your worst, you no-good, mule-lovin' bastard! I ain't afraid of you! I'll—"

"Shut up," said a voice. It didn't belong to Slocum, Mace thought, but he supposed he could have been wrong, given the shape he was in. "I'm not Slocum," the voice continued. "But you look like a man with a grudge against him, which means I'm going to patch you up and let you ride with me, as long as it doesn't take too much time." The man knelt beside Mace. "You see, I want to find Slocum too."

"Wha . . . what for?"

"I plan on killing him . . . sooner or later."

Mace lifted his trembling hand and clasped the hand the

man extended to him. "I'm . . . with you, pard," he rasped. "I'm sure as hell with you on that."

In the moonlight, after they had rounded up all the horses and made camp, Slocum dug a bottle of whiskey out of the supplies and poured it over the bullet graze on his arm. He gritted his teeth against the fiery sensation, then wrapped a strip of clean cloth around the wound and knotted it tightly with Delaney's help. Those precautions would be plenty to keep the shallow gash from festering, if he was lucky.

Delaney gnawed on some leftover biscuits and a strip of jerky. He gestured down the slope toward the dark, sprawled shapes that were the dead buffalo hunters. "What do we do about them?" he asked.

Slocum had already spotted other shapes—low, quick-moving, furred shapes—darting around the bodies. The faint sound of growling drifted through the night air as the pack of coyotes squabbled among themselves over who was going to take first crack at these delicacies. With a small, grim smile, Slocum said, "Don't reckon we'll have to worry about them. They'll likely be gone by morning . . . most of them anyway."

He had already stripped the bodies of all the weapons, ammunition, money, and other valuables they'd been carrying. The coyotes were welcome to what was left as far as he was concerned. Slocum wasn't going to lose any sleep over men who had tried to kill him. Later, the buzzards could pick the bones clean, and that would be just fine with him too.

"The West is really a barbaric place, isn't it?" said Delaney, sounding disgusted as the growling and snapping from down below grew louder.

"No, it's just fair," Slocum said. "Most of the world isn't like that. But out here, if a man is good enough to do what he sets out to do, he lives. If he's not, he dies. Fair and simple."

Delaney didn't make any reply to that, and Slocum was glad. He was tired and his arm hurt, and he didn't want to sit around and argue philosophy with some lame-brained St. Louis pilgrim.

By the next morning, Slocum's arm was a little stiff, but other than that it seemed to be fine. Just as he had expected, the scavengers had dragged off the bodies during the night. Slocum regretted losing the Appaloosa; it had been a good mount. But he picked out a rangy buckskin from among the horses that had been ridden by the buffalo hunters, and by the time the sun was beginning to peek over the horizon to their left, he and Delaney were heading south again.

A couple of days later the landscape, which had been largely flat and almost featureless ever since they had left Tascosa, grew more rugged. In some places the ground fell away almost a thousand feet to broad, brush-dotted, flat-bottomed canyons. Of course, as Slocum pointed out, these weren't all separate canyons but rather winding branches of the main canyon known as Palo Duro.

There was another significant change. They began seeing clumps of cattle, a mixture of longhorns, Durham, and Hereford. "We're on JA range now," Slocum told Delaney. "It's the biggest ranch in this part of the country. Run by a gent named Goodnight and named after his partner, an Englishman called John Adair."

"You know them?" asked Delaney.

"I know Goodnight. Used to ride for him and Oliver Loving, back before the Comanches killed Loving, and Goodnight came up here to the Panhandle and threw in with Adair. Never met Adair. I hear tell that he doesn't like to come out here, that he's content to let Goodnight run things."

Delaney snorted in contempt. "Neglecting an investment like that is a good way to get fleeced."

Slocum gave him a slit-eyed look and said, "I wouldn't go hinting that Charley Goodnight would steal from a partner. Not while we're on JA range anyway."

"No offense meant," Delaney said hurriedly.

"You don't have to worry about offending *me*. But Goodnight and his men might not take kindly to talk like that."

They rode on, descending into the canyon as it widened even more and encountering more and more cattle. By late afternoon, Slocum had spotted a thin spiral of smoke climbing into the sky. That would be from the cookshack at ranch head-quarters, he figured. By evening, lights were visible ahead of them. They kept riding until they reached a sprawling adobe house surrounded by barns, corrals, a bunkhouse, a cookshack, a powder magazine, and other outbuildings.

"It's quite a spread now," Slocum said with a grin as he pulled rein in front of the house. A dog was barking at them from the porch. Over the barking, Slocum continued. "When Goodnight moved out here a few years ago, there was nothing but a cedar-pole shack chinked with mud."

The door of the house opened and a man stepped out. Slo-cum had already seen movement at the bunkhouse door and knew that a man stood there too, a rifle trained on the visitors. There were probably several other guns pointing at them from various locations around the ranch headquarters. Charley Goodnight hadn't lived as long as he had by being careless, and neither had the men who rode for him.

In the light from the house, the man on the porch was re-vealed to be medium-sized, with a straight back, a shock of dark hair, and a neatly trimmed goatee. A rifle was tucked under his left arm, not threatening, but handy if he needed it. "Who's there?" he called in a firm, resonant voice.

"It's John Slocum, Cap. I rode with you and Mr. Loving out to Fort Sumner a few years back."

Charles Goodnight stepped out from under the awning over the porch. "I remember you, Slocum. You were a good hand, if I recollect right. Heard you've had a few scrapes with the authorities since those days."

Slocum shrugged. "The law and I haven't always seen eye to eye on everything," he admitted.

"Not running from a badge-toter right now, are you?"

"No, sir, I'm not," Slocum answered honestly.

"Then you're welcome on the JA," said Goodnight, accepting Slocum's word without hesitation. "Who's that with you?"

Delaney reached up and tugged on the brim of his derby. "My name is Calvin Delaney, Mr. Goodnight. Mr. Slocum and I are traveling together."

Goodnight grunted. "Not from these parts, are you?"

"No, sir. St. Louis."

"Well, light and set, the both of you. You're too late for supper, but I reckon we can scrape something up."

Several cowboys appeared out of the shadows as Slocum and Delaney swung down from their saddles. "We'll take care of the hosses," one of them said to Slocum, and he nodded in appreciation. Goodnight had already turned away and was going back in the house. Slocum and Delaney followed.

A thin-faced but attractive middle-aged woman joined Goodnight in greeting the two visitors in a low-ceilinged parlor furnished with heavy chairs and woven rugs. A stone fireplace stood on one side of the room, and mounted on the wall above it was a magnificent spread of longhorns. The woman smiled at Slocum and Delaney, who took off their hats. "Good evening, gentlemen," she said.

"Slocum, you remember my wife Molly," Goodnight said.

"No, sir, I think you and the lady got hitched after I rode for you." Slocum smiled at Molly Goodnight. "But I'm pleased and honored to make your acquaintance, ma'am."

"Come into the dining room," Molly said. "I've sent Jerry Shea out to the cookshack to see what he can find." She quirked an eyebrow at her husband. "Mr. Shea was rather inebriated, Charles. You're going to have to do something about him someday."

Goodnight sighed. "I know, dear, I know. But he's the best man with a chuckwagon I've ever seen. I'd hate to lose him."

"Whatever you've got will be fine with us," Slocum assured the Goodnights. "We'll just be glad to sit down to a warm meal again, won't we, Delaney?"

"Yes indeed," Delaney agreed.

"We have some other guests at the moment, friends of John

Adair's from Chicago," Goodnight said, "but they've already turned in for the evening."

Slocum nodded, not surprised at what Goodnight had said. Easterners liked to come out here to the West and pretend they were pioneers for a few days . . . before going back to their soft, pampered lives in more civilized country.

Goodnight went on. "What brings you to the JA, Slocum?"

Before Slocum could answer, Molly Goodnight murmured, "I'll just go see how Mr. Shea is doing with that meal. Excuse me, gentlemen."

Slocum and Delaney both gave her polite nods as she left the room. Obviously, it was her habit to make herself scarce when the menfolk started to talk business.

"Delaney and I aren't just drifting, Cap," Slocum said.

"I thought as much. Drink?"

The offer brought nods from both visitors. As he moved over toward a carved side table with several bottles on it, Goodnight said, "Go on."

"We're looking for someone," Slocum said, with a look at Delaney that meant *Let me do the talking*. "A woman, probably traveling alone except for a baby. She's young, blond, and pretty. The woman, that is, not the baby. He's a boy named Edgar, about a year old. The woman calls herself Rose."

Goodnight poured whiskey in three glasses and handed one each to Slocum and Delaney. With a frown, he asked, "What would a woman be doing traveling through this wilderness with only a mere babe for company? Is the child hers?"

Delaney spoke up, ignoring Slocum's earlier look. "Hers and mine, Mr. Goodnight. Rose is my wife, and Edgar is our son. We got separated while we were up in the Panhandle, headed for New Mexico Territory. I met Mr. Slocum in Tascosa, and he kindly agreed to help me look for my family."

"I see," Goodnight said. He sipped his drink.

There was something in Goodnight's eyes that Slocum didn't like. It hadn't been there before, but it was now.

Suspicion.

But what the hell had he or Delaney said that would make the cattle baron wary of them? There was nothing about a missing wife and baby that ought to arouse anyone's suspicions.

"This is a bit odd, gentlemen," Goodnight said slowly. Slocum's hand tightened on his glass. He hadn't taken a drink of the whiskey yet, and he didn't plan to until he figured out what was happening here. Warning bells were going off in his brain.

"What's odd about it, Cap?" he asked.

"Our other visitors . . . they're looking for a baby too."

The words were barely out of Goodnight's mouth when a woman came through one of the doors into the parlor. Slocum turned, saw pale skin, a tumble of red hair, and the deepest green eyes he had ever encountered.

"A baby!" she repeated breathlessly. There was a desperate, ragged edge in her voice as she went on. "Oh, Charles, have you had word about that poor precious little child?"

12

Slocum bit back the curse that sprang to his lips. He had lived a long, eventful life, but never in all his days had he run into so many people who were looking for babies. The whole damn State of Texas had gone baby-crazy.

Despite the worry lines etched on her face, the woman who had just come into the room was well worth looking at. Slocum figured she was within a year or two of thirty, one way or the other, and her clear, smooth skin and expensive gown told him that she had lived those years in wealthy surroundings. Her red hair fell to her shoulders in a mass of dense ringlets, framing a lovely face. The dark green dress she wore, which almost matched her eyes, was cut low enough so that the swells of high, full breasts were enticingly visible. She was breathing hard with excitement, which made it difficult not to look at those breasts, Slocum thought.

Charles Goodnight said, "Gentlemen, this is Mrs. Steven Mulwray. Mrs. Mulwray, Mr. Slocum and Mr. Delaney."

Both men nodded to her. "Ma'am," Delaney said. Something in his voice made Slocum glance over at him, and he saw that Delaney was gazing in open, almost lustful admiration at Mrs. Mulwray. That brought a frown to Slocum's face. A man who was searching for his missing wife and child shouldn't be looking at another woman like that.

Mrs. Mulwray didn't seem to notice. She ignored Slocum and Delaney, looking again at Goodnight and saying, "I heard voices out here, and then I heard you mention something about a baby. Have you heard anything?"

"I'm not sure," Goodnight replied. He inclined his head toward Slocum and Delaney. "These two men are looking for a woman and a baby. Perhaps the object of their search is the same as yours."

That got the redheaded Mrs. Mulwray's attention. She turned those wide green eyes toward Slocum and Delaney and asked, "Do you know anything about Kenneth?"

"Kenneth?" repeated Slocum.

"My nephew," Mrs. Mulwray said, her voice trembling with that rough edge of strain again. "The only child of my poor departed brother-in-law and sister-in-law."

Delaney shook his head. "I'm sorry, ma'am." He seemed a bit less overwhelmed now by Mrs. Mulwray's beauty. "We're looking for my boy Edgar and my wife Rose."

"Oh!" The exclamation from Mrs. Mulwray was one of disappointment. "For a moment there, I . . . I thought you might know something about Kenneth."

Slocum wanted to scratch his head in confusion, but he reined in the impulse. He wasn't the only one who was puzzled. Goodnight said, "You mean there are *two* missing babies here in the Panhandle? Good God!"

Slocum felt like echoing that sentiment. Instead he said, "Maybe if you could tell us a little about your nephew, Mrs. Mulwray . . . ?"

She nodded. Then her eyes fastened on the untouched drink in Goodnight's hand. "Charles, if you don't mind, I think some spirits might fortify me and enable me to describe once again the ordeal Steven and I have been through."

"Of course," Goodnight murmured. He started to hand her his drink, then decided to fix a fresh one and went over to the side table.

Meanwhile, Mrs. Mulwray looked at Slocum and Delaney and said, "You see, gentlemen, a few weeks ago my nephew was kidnapped from the home I share in Chicago with my husband Steven.''

''The baby's parents are dead?'' Slocum asked bluntly, remembering what she had said earlier about her departed brother-in-law and sister-in-law. Slocum didn't think she meant they'd left town.

Mrs. Mulwray nodded again. ''That's right. They were killed in a terrible accident about six months ago. They were sailing on the lake, and their boat went down. After that, Steven and I took little Kenneth into our home to raise as our own, of course. Steven and his younger brother Willis were the only members of their family left alive, so Kenneth had no one else except us.'' A bittersweet smile curved her full red lips. ''But in that six months we learned to love the child just as much as if he had been our own. That's why it was such a horrible blow when he was kidnapped.''

''Why would anybody want to kidnap a baby?'' asked Delaney. ''That's about the lowest thing I've ever heard!''

''Money,'' Mrs. Mulwray said. ''The abductors are holding him for ransom.''

Slocum had figured that out even before Mrs. Mulwray answered. There was no other reason anybody would grab a kid, at least not that he could see.

''I'm mighty sorry to hear about your problems, ma'am,'' he said to the woman.

''So am I,'' added Delaney. ''I know what it's like to not know if you'll ever see your baby again.''

Awareness of someone else's plight seemed to dawn in Mrs. Mulwray's eyes. ''I'm sorry, Mr. . . . Delaney, was it? You're in the midst of your own tragedy, aren't you? What happened to your wife and child?''

''We were traveling to Santa Fe,'' Delaney explained. ''We got separated, and then a storm hit and I couldn't find Rose or little Edgar. . . .'' His voice cracked a little, and he had to swallow before he could go on. ''I've been looking for them ever since, for over a week now. Mr. Slocum is helping me. We think Rose is headed south with the baby.''

Delaney had left out any mention of the argument that had prompted Rose to leave him in the first place, Slocum noted. But he supposed it wouldn't hurt to leave the man a little shred of dignity. Delaney was already blaming himself for whatever might have happened to Rose and Edgar. He didn't need everybody else pointing fingers of guilt at him.

Mrs. Mulwray took the glass of brandy Goodnight brought to her and swallowed a sip of it, then managed to smile slightly. "How old is your son?" she asked Delaney.

"Almost a year. Cute little fella with brown hair."

"Kenneth is about the same age, but his hair is very pale, almost white. My husband says that all the boys in his family had hair like that, that it never darkened until they were all eight or nine years old."

"Some kids are like that, Mrs. Mulwray, or so I've heard."

"Please, call me Sheila."

Slocum listened to the exchange and heard the undercurrent of tension and fear under the mundane words. Delaney and Sheila Mulwray were both afraid that they would never see their sons again, he thought. Kenneth Mulwray wasn't really Sheila's son, but it was clear she regarded the boy as her own.

"Well, this is an odd coincidence," Goodnight said again, "but I suppose after living in Texas this long I shouldn't be surprised by anything I run into. I reckon there have been plenty of babies lost out here at one time or another." He looked at Sheila Mulwray and added quickly, "And I'm sure most of them were found safe and sound."

Slocum wasn't convinced of that at all. The frontier was a dangerous enough place without throwing in some kidnappers on top of it. He was curious about something, so after he had taken a sip of the whiskey Goodnight had poured for him, he asked Sheila, "What brings you and your husband out here to the JA, ma'am? Do you think you'll find your nephew here?"

"Steven hired detectives, of course, when Kenneth was abducted," Sheila said. "They tracked the kidnappers all the way to Wichita, Kansas, before they lost the trail. When Kenneth was . . . taken . . . the men left a note saying that they would be in touch with us, and we received a letter that was mailed from Wichita. It instructed us to gather fifty thousand dollars and give it to someone we trusted who was to bring it to El Paso, Texas. Our courier would be contacted there, and Kenneth would be returned safely when the money was turned over to the kidnappers.'' She drew a deep, shaky breath. ''Steven was . . . not inclined to cooperate to such an extent.''

''He's not going to pay the ransom?'' Delaney asked in surprise.

''Not unless he's forced to. You see, later the detectives received a report that Kenneth had been spotted in Indian Territory. He was with two men who were heading west.''

''The kidnappers,'' Slocum said. ''They were bound for El Paso for the rendezvous.''

Sheila nodded. ''That's what Steven thinks. He decided that we would come down here to Texas and try to intercept those horrible men who stole Kenneth. We know John Adair, and he suggested that we stop over here at the ranch he and Mr. Goodnight own while our detectives scour the plains for any sign of Kenneth's kidnappers.''

The wheels of Slocum's brain were clicking over like those of a fast-moving locomotive. Some of the things that had baffled him before were starting to make at least a little sense. That gunman in the duster back in Tascosa could have been one of the detectives working for the Mulwrays. The object of his search could have been Kenneth Mulwray, rather than Edgar Delaney. But when he had heard that some drifter was in town looking for a baby, he could have jumped to the conclusion that Slocum was connected to the kidnappers.

Yeah, that theory held water, Slocum decided. The gunman hadn't looked or acted much like a detective, but that didn't really mean anything. The Pinkertons employed a wide variety of men as agents, and so did the other detective agencies. Slocum remembered running into a pair of Pinkertons who hadn't looked or acted much like detectives either. One of them was a derby-hatted dude who drove a phony medicine wagon, and the other was some sort of hillbilly gunfighter from Arkansas. They hadn't been above bending a few rules when they had to in order to get the results they wanted.

"And you're welcome to stay as long as you want, Mrs. Mulwray," Goodnight was saying. "I know Molly enjoys having you here and hearing about everything that's going on back East."

Sheila gave the rancher a wan smile. "I'm sure that if we don't have any luck with our search soon, Steven will want to move on to El Paso in hopes of finding the kidnappers there."

"But he *is* going to pay the ransom if he has to, isn't he?" asked Delaney. "I'd hate to think about that poor baby being in the hands of those thieves if they don't get what they want."

"He'll pay," Sheila said firmly. "I'll insist on it."

Slocum was willing to bet that she would get her way too. Not many men would be able to say no to a woman who looked like Sheila Mulwray—especially a man who was married to her.

Slocum became aware that Sheila was studying him rather intently. He didn't know whether to be uncomfortable or flattered. After a moment, she said, "Mr. Slocum, are you and Mr. Delaney related?"

"Nope," Slocum said.

"Good friends perhaps?"

Slocum glanced at Delaney, wondering what the man was hoping he would say in reply to that question. Slocum told the truth. "No, we never met until a few days ago."

"Then why are you helping him search for his family?"

"I ran into Mrs. Delaney and the boy up north of Tascosa and helped keep them from freezing to death in a blue norther. Then Mrs. Delaney left camp while I was asleep. She took a good horse of mine with her."

Goodnight chuckled. "So you're hunting a horse as much as you are the woman and the child, John?"

"I wouldn't say that, Cap. I want to make sure Mrs. Delaney and Edgar are all right. But I'd like to have that dun horse back too."

Sheila nodded. "Oh. I see. I was hoping that perhaps I could persuade you to help us look for Kenneth."

A frown appeared on Slocum's face. The Mulwrays were evidently willing to pay quite well for someone to find that baby. And he wasn't making a damn thing for riding along with Calvin Delaney. Of course, Delaney had offered to pay him for his help, but all anybody had to do was look at Delaney to know that the pilgrim didn't have even a fraction of the money Sheila and her husband did. He could abandon the search for Rose and go to work for the Mulwrays, and even if he didn't find little Kenneth—which seemed pretty likely— he would probably make enough money to keep him comfortably in San Antonio until spring. It was something to think about. . . .

But then he heard himself saying, "I'm sorry, Mrs. Mulwray, but I don't reckon I'd better take on another chore until I finish the one I've got now."

"You're sure?"

Slocum nodded. Beside him, Delaney looked considerably relieved. Obviously, he hadn't liked the idea of being left on his own out here.

"Well, I'm sorry you feel that way, but I understand," Sheila said. She turned to Delaney and laid a hand on his arm. "I hope you find your wife and child, Mr. Delaney. I really do."

"Thank you, ma'am," Delaney said.

She lifted the glass of brandy Goodnight had given her and drank the rest of it. "I'll say good night now, gentlemen. I had already retired for the evening, but when I heard your horses come in, I hoped it might be some of the detectives returning."

"I'm sorry there was no good news," said Goodnight.

Sheila smiled sadly. "I'm sure there will be, sooner or later."

She turned and left the room through the door by which she had entered. Slocum, Delaney, and Goodnight watched her go, and when the door was closed behind her, Goodnight shook his head and said, "It's a terrible shame. I can't imagine anybody putting a youngster's life in danger like that."

"Some men will do almost anything for money, Cap," Slocum said.

Goodnight looked at him shrewdly and said, "Some might even say that you fit into that category, John, considering some of the stories I've heard about you. But I know better. You'd never threaten a child."

Slocum shrugged, but he knew Goodnight was right. It had been difficult turning down Sheila Mulwray's request for help. The only reason he'd been able to do it was the knowledge that Rose Delaney and Edgar might need him even more.

Molly Goodnight came back into the room. "Supper is on the table, gentlemen," she announced.

Slocum grinned. "I'm ready for it. It's been a long, hard ride."

And he wondered just where and when it was going to end.

13

Slocum and Delaney ate their fill while Charles Goodnight sat at the table with them in the big dining room and smoked a cigar. The conversation between Slocum and Goodnight was peppered with references to old friends and enemies. Delaney listened intently as he ate, and finally he said, "You two know just about everybody who's famous out here in the West, don't you?"

"The frontier may stretch for thousands of miles," Goodnight said, "but in a way it's like a small community, Mr. Delaney. There aren't that many people out here, so we tend to keep running into each other as we move around. And a fellow like John here, who's restless by nature, encounters even more people than most."

Slocum grinned as he chewed a bite of the huge pan-fried steak that had been on his plate. "What the cap'n is saying is that I don't stay in one place too long."

"For health reasons, I'm sure," Goodnight added dryly.

Slocum's grin widened, even though he was thinking of all the times he'd nearly had his neck stretched by vigilance committees or just plain lynch mobs. Goodnight was right; there wasn't anything much more unhealthy than that.

When the meal was over, Goodnight offered cigars to both of his new visitors, as well as glasses of brandy. Slocum enjoyed the smoke, but between the whiskey he had drunk earlier, the heavy meal, and the smooth but potent brandy, he found his eyelids drooping and his head sagging toward his chest after only a short time. Stifling a yawn with his hand, he said, "I'm about ready to turn in."

Delaney nodded. His face was drawn, almost gaunt with weariness. "Me too."

"I can put you up here in the house if you'd like," offered Goodnight. "Or if you'd prefer, you can sleep in the bunkhouse with the hands."

Slocum figured most of the JA cowboys had already gone to bed. Even though there weren't as many tasks to take care of on a ranch at this time of year, he knew the hands would be up before dawn the next morning anyway. He didn't want to disturb their rest.

"If you've got the room, I'll bunk here in the house," he said to Goodnight.

The cattle baron nodded. "Sure. Molly's retired already, so I'll show you where to pitch your soogans."

He led them down a hallway in the sprawling ranch house and pointed out two doors made of heavy wood, one on each side of the corridor. "These are guest rooms," Goodnight said. "Take your pick."

Slocum inclined his head toward the door on the left. "I'll take this one."

"Fine with me," Delaney said. "I don't care where the room is, as long as it's got a bed in it."

Goodnight clamped his teeth on another cigar and nodded to Slocum and Delaney. They went into the rooms.

Slocum found the guest room on the left to be small but comfortably furnished. There was a bed with a woven spread on it, a rug on the floor, a ladderback chair, and a heavy wardrobe of polished oak. The shutters were closed on the room's single window. A candle sat in a silver holder on top of the wardrobe. Slocum scratched a lucifer into life and lit it before he closed the door.

The bed looked mighty appealing. He shucked out of his

clothes quickly, dragging the chair over beside the bed so that he could place his coiled gunbelt and the holstered Colt Navy on it. Then, wearing only his long-handled underwear, he blew out the candle and threw himself on the bed.

Sleep claimed him almost before his head hit the pillow. For a while, he slumbered soundly, deep in a dreamless sleep. But then he grew more restless, stirring in the bed as dreams crept in and started tormenting his defenseless brain. He kept seeing two babies toddling along in front of him. He hurried to catch up to them, thinking he had found Edgar Delaney and Kenneth Mulwray, but even when he broke into a run, his long-legged strides didn't bring him even with the children. Somehow, despite their unsteady gait, they stayed ahead of him. In his dream, Slocum bellowed, "Wait just a damned minute!" at them, but they didn't stop, didn't even slow down.

Suddenly, he wasn't running anymore. He was on top of that lineback dun Rose Delaney had stolen from him, and he was galloping after the babies. He didn't know where the horse had come from, but with the unwavering confidence of dreams, he didn't even ponder the question. Surely he could catch them now, he thought. There was no way a couple of toddlers could outrun a horse.

But instead of closing the gap, he realized the babies were getting farther and farther in front of him. Slocum cursed. They were going to get away from him, and there wasn't a blasted thing he could do about it.

Then, as suddenly as the babies had pulled away from him, they stopped in their tracks. In fact, they turned and came toward him, and Slocum felt relief wash over him.

Until he realized that each of the babies was holding a six-gun in a chubby little hand.

"Damn it, they're armed!" Slocum exclaimed in his dream-world, unaware that he was tossing and turning in the bed and groaning.

Not only were the little devils armed, they were raising those guns and pointing them at him, and to his horror, the muzzles of the revolvers began to belch flame and smoke as the babies started shooting at him. He was plunging ahead, right into that hail of gunfire, and there was nothing he could do about it—

Slocum jerked over onto his back and started to sit up, a yell forming on his lips. Before it could escape, a hand closed over his mouth, and a voice hissed urgently, "Ssshhh! Please, Mr. Slocum, don't cry out!"

The palm of the hand pressed to his lips was smooth and soft, and so was the hand that closed on his shoulder. His eyes widened in the darkness. A faint but fragrant smell of perfume came to him, and he could feel the warmth of the body that was perched close to him on the edge of the bed.

The hand over his mouth went away, and in the darkness Sheila Mulwray said in a half whisper, "My goodness, Mr. Slocum, you startled me! I didn't mean to frighten you."

Slocum grimaced. Keeping his own voice pitched low so that it wouldn't travel, he said, "I wasn't scared of you, Mrs. Mulwray. I was having a bad dream. But I'm mighty puzzled."

He felt the warmth of her breath against his cheek. She was that close to him as she said, "Puzzled about what?"

"What you're doing here," Slocum said bluntly.

She still had a hand on his shoulder. She ran it down over his chest, then moved it to his arm. When she found his hand, she grasped his wrist and lifted it, guiding his hand to her body. His fingers closed around the smooth firmness of a pear-shaped breast, its nipple erect.

"Isn't it obvious?" asked Sheila.

Slocum's jaw tightened, and that wasn't all. His manhood was beginning to stiffen. He tightened his grip on Sheila's breast. It was the left one, he decided. He lifted his other hand to the right one and caressed it as well. He suspected she was naked, and when he pulled her closer to him, the feel of her body as she molded it to his confirmed that guess.

Slocum had never been one to think a thing to death. A beautiful naked woman shows up in your bedroom in the middle of the night, you do what comes naturally. That was his philosophy.

But he couldn't quite forget that this particular beautiful naked woman was somebody else's wife. Not only that, but she was searching for a kidnapped child and had seemed mighty upset about the whole thing earlier. She hadn't acted like getting into bed with John Slocum had been on her mind at all.

Her lips found his in the darkness. Her mouth was wet and open and wanting. His tongue met hers. They circled and danced, probed and thrust. Slocum's shaft was so hard now it was tenting out painfully against the long underwear.

Sheila took care of that. Her nimble fingers quickly undid his buttons, freeing the long, thick pole of flesh. They closed hotly around it, and even though her mouth was still plastered to his, she gave a moan of appreciation deep in her throat as she measured the length and breadth of him.

Slocum broke the kiss and said hoarsely, "As good as it feels to have you rubbing my pecker like that, Mrs. Mulwray, I'd still like to know what you're doing here."

She gasped, and Slocum hoped he hadn't offended her so badly that she was going to jump off the bed and flounce out of the room. "Why do you *think* I'm here?" she asked tautly.

"Could be you thought I might take you up on that job offer if you sweetened the pot a little."

For a moment, she didn't say anything. Then, surprising Slocum, she gave a little laugh. "My, but you have a high opinion of yourself, don't you, Mr. Slocum?" she said. "You think that I want your help so badly that I have to sacrifice my honor to entice you into helping my husband and myself. But that's not it at all."

"It's not?" Slocum said.

"No." Sheila still had one of her hands wrapped around his shaft. She began to slowly slide it up and down. "You see, we already have some excellent detectives working for us, Mr. Slocum. What I want from you is this, and only this." Her hand tightened on him. "My husband is considerably older than me. Steven is fifty. Most of the time, he's unable to perform his husbandly duties, and even when he manages to try, he fails to satisfy me. And I'm a woman of . . . healthy appetites, Mr. Slocum.''

"Nothing wrong with that, I reckon," Slocum said. "But under the circumstances—"

"You mean because of Kenneth?" The strain he had heard earlier crept back into her voice. "You're right, of course. I should be worried about him and not even thinking about . . . well, about this." Again she caressed him. "But different people react differently to such painful situations. I need something to take my mind off everything. I need to be able to forget all my troubles, even if it's only for a few minutes." She laughed again. "You're nothing but a distraction, Mr. Slocum. But you're a very virile, attractive man, and I knew as soon as I saw you that you could provide a very welcome diversion for me."

"You're a cold-blooded bitch, aren't you?" Slocum growled the words between clenched teeth.

He felt her moving, changing position, and then she said in the darkness, "No, I'm a *hot-blooded* bitch."

Her lips closed around the head of his shaft and she began to suck.

Slocum admired honesty in a woman. And while he might not have any particular fondness for Sheila Mulwray, he had to admit that she was damned good at what she was doing to him. He buried his fingers in her hair, enjoying the feel of that silky red mass as he gripped her head and thrust in and out of her mouth. She moaned in sheer lustful abandon.

She wanted a diversion, did she? Wanted her mind on nothing else but what Slocum was doing to her? He would try to oblige.

Pulling out of her mouth while he still could, he reached out and drew her up next to him on the bed. He rolled her over onto her belly, then splayed his big hands out on her back and began massaging her, slowly working his way down to the swell of her rump. Cupping a cheek in each hand, he caressed and spread them. She opened her legs so that he could kneel between them. His fingers found the folds of flesh and toyed with them. She was already wet with need. Slocum lowered his head and ran his tongue along the gates of her femaleness.

He lapped and sucked and thrust, bringing more groans from her. Her hips worked up and down of their own volition, and her breath rasped in her throat. "Oh, John!" she cried softly. "That's so *good*!"

Slocum was glad to hear it. But he was just getting started.

He penetrated her with two fingers, stroking her as deeply as he could with them. The noises she made in response were muffled, as if she had dragged one of the pillows over to her and buried her face in it. With his other hand, Slocum caressed the valley between the cheeks of her bottom. She gave another stifled cry.

Slocum slid his fingers out of her and grasped her hips. He lifted her and moved behind her on the bed. He had to aim himself by feel in the darkness, but a moment later the head of his shaft touched her hot, wet core, and with a flicking thrust of his hips, he buried himself in her.

Sheila was the second married woman Slocum had been with recently. Both she and Rose Delaney had come to him and initiated the lovemaking, so he wasn't going to worry overmuch about the morals of it. He drove hard into Sheila, holding her hips firmly as his groin slapped into her rump with each stroke. She thrust back at him, her need making her movements frantic and spasmodic. A sharp exhalation of breath escaped from her lips each time he pistoned into her.

After a few minutes of going at it hot and heavy, Slocum slowed his pace. Holding himself still inside her, he leaned forward, sliding his hands up her flanks and underneath her to cup her breasts and pinch her nipples. That brought even more cries of passion from her, but thankfully she smothered them with the pillow or the sheet or whatever she had stuffed in her mouth. Slocum was grateful for her discretion. He didn't particularly want all of Captain Goodnight's household knowing that he had Mrs. Mulwray in his bed.

Finally, neither of them could take it anymore. Slocum straightened and once again began driving his throbbing shaft deeply into her. He caught hold of her hips and dug his thumbs into the yielding softness of her bottom. Pulling back on her as he thrust forward, he plunged into her as deeply as he possibly could and began releasing his climax in a mind-numbing series of shuddering spurts. He emptied himself into her, his juices mixing with hers in a flood that overflowed her core and soaked the sac below his shaft. She spasmed wildly around him in her own culmination.

Sheila sagged forward as if every bone in her body had turned to jelly. Slocum let go of her. He felt pretty exhausted himself. He sprawled on the bed beside her, lying on his back.

She rolled over and snuggled against him, her hands exploring his broad, thickly furred chest. "Oh, John," she whispered. "You were as good as I knew you would be when I first saw you."

Slocum chuckled. "Satisfied, were you?"

"Oh, yes. Like . . . like never before."

"You don't have to lie to me," Slocum said. "You're not a two-dollar whore telling some man he's the best she's ever had when they both know that's not true. I'm just glad I could bring you a little happiness."

"You did," said Sheila. "You certainly did. But now . . ." Her voice trailed away.

"I know. You have to go back to your husband."

"Please don't be jealous, John."

It wouldn't do any good for him to explain to her that he wasn't jealous, Slocum thought. She had a high enough opinion of her sensual skills that she automatically assumed any man lucky enough to bed her would immediately start feeling possessive toward her. Slocum didn't see any point in disillusioning her.

"Be careful," he said. "I don't want to cause trouble for Charley Goodnight."

"Neither do I. Don't worry, I'll be discreet. No one will ever know what passed between us tonight. I just wish we could see each other—like this—again." She sighed in what sounded like genuine regret. "But we both have other things to worry about, don't we? Our paths may never cross again."

"You never know what'll happen," Slocum told her, trying to sound reassuring. But he knew she was right. He had to find Rose and Edgar, and she would be leaving with her husband to continue their search for their missing nephew and the kidnappers who had stolen the boy from them.

She gave him a last kiss and slid out of bed. "Good night," she said.

"Good night," replied Slocum. He lay there motionless until he heard the door close behind her.

Then, feeling a twinge of loss, he rolled over and went back to sleep.

14

Steven and Sheila Mulwray were already eating breakfast when Slocum and Delaney walked into the dining room the next morning. There was no sign of Charles Goodnight, but since the sun was already up, that didn't surprise Slocum. Molly Goodnight was sitting at the table and sipping coffee, keeping her guests company. She had probably eaten hours earlier with her husband and the ranch hands.

When Slocum and Delaney came into the room, Steven Mulwray grunted and put down his knife and fork. He stood up and stepped around the table to greet them. "Good morning, gentlemen," he said as he shook hands with them. "My wife and Mrs. Goodnight told me there were other visitors here at the JA. I'm pleased to make your acquaintance."

"Likewise, I'm sure," Delaney said. Slocum just returned Mulwray's firm grip and gave him a nod.

Mulwray was a big man, almost as tall and broad-shouldered as Slocum. He might have been physically powerful at one time, but age had softened him some. He had a large nose, and its reddish tinge, as well as the broken veins in Mulwray's cheeks, told Slocum that the man was a heavy drinker. He had lost most of his hair, and the ring of it that was left above his ears and around the back of his head was white. His eyes were a watery blue. The suit he wore was

115

expensive and somewhat out of place here in this rustic ranch house dining room.

Slocum could understand what had drawn Sheila to Mulwray in the first place: an air of sophistication and wealth—and more importantly, the power and influence that went with it. But he could tell as well why Sheila had a roving eye and the willingness to satisfy her sensual appetites. Mulwray wasn't enough man for a woman like Sheila.

And neither was *he,* thought Slocum with a wry, inward chuckle. No one man would ever be able to take care of all her needs, at least not for long.

As Slocum and Delaney sat down at the places which had been prepared for them, Sheila said to them, "There's been no word about Kenneth. I assumed since you gentlemen were concerned about him last night, you'd want to know."

Delaney nodded. "Yes, ma'am, thank you. And we're sorry you haven't heard anything, aren't we, John?"

Slocum couldn't remember giving Delaney leave to call him by his first name. He wasn't going to say anything about it under these circumstances, however. There would be time enough later to remind Delaney that they weren't friends, just two men with a common goal riding together.

"My wife told me that she informed you of our tragic loss," said Mulwray.

"We haven't lost Kenneth yet," Sheila said sharply. "We're going to find him, Steven."

"Of course, dear, of course," Mulwray murmured.

Slocum could tell he didn't really believe it, though. Mulwray had the look and sound of a man who had already given up and admitted defeat.

"I have to admire you, sir," Delaney said to Mulwray as he helped himself to a pile of fried potatoes, some scrambled eggs, and several thick slices of ham. "I mean, for not giving in to those kidnappers' demands while trying to get your nephew back anyway. That takes courage."

Mulwray snorted in disgust. "I didn't get where I am today by letting people run over me, I can tell you that, Mr. Dela-

SLOCUM AND THE TEXAS ROSE   117

ney." He sounded as if he was on surer ground now that he was talking about himself.

"What is it you do for a living?" asked Delaney.

"My late brother and I owned one of the largest shipping firms on the Great Lakes," Mulwray said proudly. "Most of the goods that go back and forth between the United States and Canada travel on our barges."

Slocum concentrated on his food while Mulwray continued to expound on his holdings. Such things had never interested Slocum, which was the main reason he never would have been a success in business, he supposed. He would have rather been thrown into Yuma Prison than chained to a desk in an office for year after year—and he knew what he was talking about, because he had been locked up in Yuma Prison a time or two.

"Mr. Slocum." Sheila Mulwray's voice broke into his reverie. "What are your plans now?"

Slocum took a sip of his coffee, then said, "Well, since there hasn't been any sign of Mrs. Delaney and the child around these parts, I guess we'll push on south."

Delaney sighed. "There's really nothing else we can do," he said.

"But what if your wife never even came this direction?" asked Sheila.

Delaney shook his head helplessly. "I . . . I don't know. We could be getting farther and farther away from her all the time."

"She couldn't have gone north from where she left me," Slocum said. "The storm was too strong for that. I don't think she would have turned around and gone back east either, since she'd just come from that direction. She could have pushed on west for New Mexico, but it would be a long way to a settlement, and she knew Tascosa was to the south."

"But she didn't go to Tascosa," Delaney pointed out. He was looking more and more worried.

"Not that we know of." Slocum didn't want to explain the main reason he thought Rose hadn't headed west: That was the way she and her husband had been going, and she wanted to get away from Delaney. She had been determined to strike out on her own, and south was the most likely direction for her to have done that.

But coming this way had been a gamble, and Slocum knew it. If he had figured wrong, they might never find Rose and little Edgar. Much as he hated to admit it, that was a definite possibility. He had thought they would pick up her trail before now, that someone would have seen her as she passed through the Panhandle.

Still, it was too late to do anything else now. They had to push on, trusting to luck.

"I'll give our men another couple of days, and then we'll move on to El Paso," Mulwray said, even though no one had asked him what his plans were.

Delaney said, "You'll pay the ransom when you get there?"

Mulwray looked at him sharply and snapped, "What business is that of yours?"

"None at all," Delaney said quickly. "I'm just worried about that little boy, what with my own son being missing and all. . . ."

Mulwray nodded, apparently mollified by Delaney's explanation. "I suppose—as a last resort, mind you—I could consider giving those beasts what they want. But I'd rather see them strung up from a good solid tree."

That sentiment, so forcefully expressed, made Mulwray rise slightly in Slocum's estimation. Mulwray was gambling with a child's life to do what he thought was right . . . but in a way, Slocum had done the same thing.

Slocum turned to Molly Goodnight. "It's been a while since I've been through these parts, ma'am," he said. "What's the nearest settlement to the south?"

"That would be Snyder," Mrs. Goodnight replied. "There's a place called Teepee City, but it's on the trail Charles Rath laid out from Dodge City for the buffalo hunters, considerably east of here. The closest towns to Snyder are Buffalo Gap to the southeast and Fort Griffin to the east."

Slocum nodded. He didn't want to pay a visit to Fort Griffin unless he had to. There was too great a likelihood that someone in that rugged frontier settlement would recognize him, since the last time he'd been there he'd gotten involved in a mix-up involving an army paymaster and a wagon load of stolen gold. Officers from the Adjutant General's office were probably still looking for him.

"There are some ranches along the way too," Molly Goodnight added. "I'm sure you and Mr. Delaney would be welcome at all of them, Mr. Slocum."

"Yes, ma'am."

"And you're welcome to replenish your supplies before you go," Molly added. "Charles and I laid in plenty for the winter. I think we could feed a small army from now until next summer if we needed to."

"We're much obliged," Slocum said. It would be good to leave the JA with full saddlebags, because it might take a week to reach Snyder, he judged. It was a long way between settlements out here on the Texas frontier.

Mulwray and Sheila finished their breakfast first and went to the parlor. When Slocum and Delaney were done, Slocum went out to the barn to check on their horses. With the extra mounts they had claimed from the dead buffalo hunters, they would be able to make good time, Slocum thought. They could switch horses frequently and push on south by southeast. He hoped they found some sign of Rose soon. Her trail would be getting colder and colder.

When Slocum came back into the house, he found Delaney sitting in the parlor with Steven Mulwray. The businessman from Chicago was saying, "We hired only the best detectives, of course, when the police couldn't help us. The Pinkertons are working for us, and I also engaged the services of a man named Kelso, who's supposed to be top-notch. They'll find those kidnappers, you can count on it, and then those bastards will be sorry they ever crossed my path."

Slocum hung his hat on a hook, shrugged out of his jacket, and indulged his curiosity by asking Mulwray, "How'd they manage to get their hands on the boy anyway?''

"My wife and I attended a party one evening, and we left young Kenneth with his governess, of course," said Mulwray. "While we were gone, two men with guns forced their way into the house, pistol-whipped the governess, and took Kenneth." His lip curled into a sneer. "Damned brutes."

"Did the woman get a good look at the kidnappers?" asked Delaney.

Mulwray shook his head. "No, they wore overcoats and hats pulled down low and masks over their faces. The woman couldn't tell the police anything about them. Of course, she was terrified and then injured. I can't blame her for not being able to describe the sons of bitches."

"Well, it's a damned shame," Delaney said. "I wish you all the luck in the world, Mr. Mulwray."

"Those kidnappers, they're the ones who'll need the luck when my men catch up to them," growled Mulwray. "And if they've hurt that boy . . ." His voice caught, and for the first time, Slocum heard something besides bluster in Mulwray's tone. "We almost lost Kenneth when Willis and Susan drowned, you know. They always took him out on the lake with them when they went sailing. The boy loves the water. But the day Willis's boat went down, Kenneth was on shore with his governess because he'd developed a cough at the last minute and Susan was afraid the excursion would make him feel worse."

"That was some good luck to go with the bad, I guess," Delaney said. "What happened to the boat? If you don't mind talking about it, that is."

Mulwray shook his head. "We don't know. We probably never will, since the boat and the bodies were never found. They're still somewhere in that damned lake." He sighed. "Willis was an excellent sailor and always kept his boat in good condition. The lake was fairly calm that day, but the boat went down anyway. I suspect it sprung a leak, and Willis wasn't able to get back to shore before it sank. A senseless tragedy if there ever was one. Willis had everything to live for—a successful business, a lovely wife and child. . . . Senseless, just senseless.''

Delaney nodded and muttered sympathetically.

Slocum left Delaney and Mulwray talking in the parlor and went to his room, thinking about what he had just heard. Mulwray had made the same mistake a lot of folks did by assuming that the world was supposed to make sense. It didn't, and Slocum had learned that a long time ago.

And yet there was something tickling at the back of Slocum's brain, a vague feeling that if he looked at things from a little different angle, they would form an entirely different picture. The sensation was faint, just strong enough to be annoying. He shook his head and tried to concentrate on other things. He and Delaney would be riding soon. They could put some more miles behind them today.

Slocum's attention was focused sharply again as soon as he stepped into his room. Sheila Mulwray was standing beside the bed, a worried frown on her face.

''I thought you'd never get here,'' she said as Slocum recovered quickly from his surprise at finding her here and closed the door behind him. She came across the room and into his arms. Slocum embraced her instinctively, and her lips found his. He returned the kiss, tasting and enjoying the hot, wet sweetness of her mouth.

But it was broad daylight now, and her husband was right down the hall. The notion of being in danger of discovery might arouse Sheila—Slocum had known some women like that—but it didn't do a damned thing for him. He broke the kiss, put his hands on her shoulders, and moved her away from him slightly.

''This isn't a good idea,'' he said in a quiet voice.

''I don't care. I've been thinking about you ever since last night. I can't think of anything else. It was torture this morning, sitting through breakfast with you right there only a few feet away. I wanted your hands on me so badly.''

Slocum smiled grimly. ''Maybe I distracted you a little too good last night.''

A sharply indrawn breath hissed between her teeth. Her hand came up, fast and hard, aimed at Slocum's face. He caught her wrist before she could slap him, the movement of his hand seeming almost lazy.

"You bastard!" she whispered.

"Never claimed to be anything else," he said.

She shuddered as the brief flash of anger faded from her green eyes. "I want you to give up this mad quest of yours and come with us," she said. "You'll never find that woman and that other child, but you *could* help us find Kenneth."

"You don't know that," said Slocum. "I haven't given up, and neither has Delaney. Besides, you've got the Pinkertons working for you. They can blanket the whole damned State of Texas and come a lot closer to finding your nephew than I can."

"Perhaps you're right." Her tongue licked over her lips. "But none of them can make me feel like you do."

Slocum wasn't so sure about that. That hillbilly Pinkerton he'd met had had quite a reputation with the ladies. . . .

But that didn't matter. He said, "I'm sorry, Sheila. You make the offer mighty appealing, but I just can't do it."

She looked like she wanted to argue with him some more, but then she sighed and nodded. "I was afraid I couldn't convince you, but I had to try. I couldn't have lived with myself if I hadn't at least asked you." She smiled faintly up at him. "You know I'm going to be awfully restless for the next few nights, don't you?"

"Maybe you ought to give your husband another chance," suggested Slocum.

Sheila looked thoughtful. "Maybe," she said. Slocum wasn't convinced she would follow his advice, though. She leaned closer to him and came up on her toes. Her fingers tangled in the thick black hair at the back of his neck. "In the meantime, I don't want you to forget me."

She kissed him again, and the heat and passion of the kiss coursed all the way through him. It was almost like being struck by lightning, Slocum thought as he put his arms around her and pressed her body to his. Not that he had ever actually been hit by lightning, of course—but he figured it had to be something like kissing Sheila Mulwray.

Then she slipped out of his arms and with a last solemn, almost sorrowful glance left the room. Slocum stood there and watched the door close behind her and thought that there was one thing she didn't have to worry about.

He wasn't likely to forget her, not any time soon.

15

Snyder had started out as a trading post set up to serve the buffalo hunters, and it wasn't much more than that now. Slocum and Delaney rode up to the big log building five days after leaving the JA Ranch in Palo Duro Canyon. It had taken a couple of days less than Slocum had estimated to reach the settlement, which consisted of the trading post and half-a-dozen other log and adobe buildings scattered along a rutted street. The ruts had been made by the wheels of wagons heavily loaded with buffalo hides. Slocum saw a large stack of the hides behind the trading post, no doubt waiting to be taken east to Fort Griffin and sold to the hide buyers there.

The trading post had a low awning in front of it supported on cedar posts with the bark peeled off. A plank sign hung from the awning, and burned into the wood in straggling letters were the words *Snyder's Tradin Post an Mercanteel—W. H. Snyder, Prop.*

Slocum reined in and swung down from his saddle. Delaney dismounted as well, and the two of them quickly tied the reins of all the horses to the hitch rack in front of the trading post. Delaney wore an eager, anxious expression. He said, "Do you think she'll be here, John? Do you think she really might be?"

Slocum never had gotten around to saying anything to Delaney about that first-name business, and by now it seemed like a waste of time to make an issue of it. Anyway, like Delaney, Slocum had other things on his mind. More important things.

Two days earlier, they had picked up Rose's trail at last.

The breakthrough had come at a small, isolated ranch on the Double Mountain Fork of the Brazos River. The ranch was run by a pair of middle-aged brothers named Brewer and their two old-maid sisters. The Brewers struck Slocum as a strange bunch, but they were friendly enough, and they admitted right away that a pretty young blonde with a year-old baby had stopped there several days earlier. She had been riding a horse that was unmistakably that lineback dun of Slocum's. Slocum wondered what had happened to the other horse. It could have run off during Rose's long trek down from the Panhandle, he supposed, or stepped in a hole and broken its leg. Texas, as the old saying went, was hell on women and horses.

"She told us her name was Rose, and she called the little boy Edgar," one of the Brewer sisters told Slocum and Delaney. "Said they'd been traveling for quite a while, but that was all."

"We ain't ones to pry in what ain't none of our business," said one of the brothers. "That's why we come out here in the middle of nowhere to start this ranch."

"So we didn't ask any questions, just accepted what she told us and fed her and the baby and that horse of theirs. They slept in the barn and moved on the next morning."

"Did she say where she was bound?" Delaney asked anxiously.

The other brother scratched his beard and said, "Not to speak of. But when she left here, she was a-headin' straight toward Snyder."

Slocum was relieved that his instincts had proven to be correct, and he was glad they were closing in on Rose at last. Other than that, he didn't take any great pleasure from the news. He hadn't decided what he would do when and if he and Delaney caught up to Rose. The simplest outcome would be if she was happy to be reunited with her husband and didn't

say anything about what had gone on that night she had spent
with Slocum during the blue norther. If that was the case, he
would keep his mouth shut too, reclaim that dun horse, and
let the Delaney family go on wherever they chose.

But what if Rose didn't want to stay with her husband? The
way she had been running for the past couple of weeks made
that seem more likely. For all Slocum knew, Delaney had mis-
treated his wife, although he seemed almost too spineless for
that. Other than during the fight with the buffalo hunters, when
Delaney's actions had been motivated by pure terror and
guided by sheer dumb luck, he hadn't shown any signs of
having much backbone. Of course, Slocum had mused more
than once, how much backbone did it take to mistreat a woman
and a baby? Not a whole hell of a lot, he had decided. But all
he knew for sure was that if Rose didn't want to stay with
Delaney, he wasn't going to force her to. He wouldn't let
Delaney force her either.

So now, here they were in Snyder, and it was possible they
would find Rose inside the trading post. Slocum had already
looked at all the horses tied up at the buildings along the rough
street, and he hadn't seen the dun. But that didn't mean it
wasn't here somewhere, maybe in a shed behind one of the
buildings.

"I don't know whether she's here or not," Slocum told
Delaney in answer to the pilgrim's anxious question. "Only
one way to find out. Let's go."

He stepped over to the door of the trading post, Delaney
following closely behind him.

Inside, the place smelled of buffalo hides, brine, tobacco
smoke, stale beer, piss, and human flesh that hadn't seen a
bathtub or even a pond for many a month. That was typical,
thought Slocum. Also typical were the low, beamed ceiling
and the narrow aisles between shelves crammed with a mind-
boggling assortment of goods for sale or trade. The store also
served as a saloon. A bar made of broad planks laid across
the tops of whiskey barrels ran across the back of the room.
A couple of kerosene lanterns that smoked and sizzled pro-

vided light, since there were no windows in the trading post.

Slocum had paused in the doorway to let his eyes grow accustomed to the dimness within the building. He didn't like that; it made him a perfect target, silhouetted against the sunlight from outside. But he liked even less the idea of walking into the trading post while he was still half blind. His vision adjusted quickly, and he looked around the room, seeing perhaps a dozen men but no women. About half of the men were standing at the bar, while a couple sat at a roughly hewn table, and the others were scattered through the trading post. Most paused in whatever they were doing to look toward the open door and the newcomers.

A man who stood behind the bar called to them, "Come in, gents, come on in. Welcome to Snyder's."

Slocum moved on into the room and motioned for Delaney to follow him. Delaney started to, and Slocum looked back and said, "Shut the door first."

"Oh. Right," said Delaney. He reached back to pull the door closed behind him.

As Slocum moved toward the bar, he had to pass close beside the table where two people sat drinking out of an earthen jug they passed back and forth. He had been wrong in his original assumption, he saw. There was a woman here in the trading post. He had taken both the drinkers at the table to be men, but one of them was female. The small breasts that pushed out against the homespun shirt under the open buffalo-hide coat and the lack of an Adam's apple gave it away. The woman's dingy brown hair was either cut very short or crammed tightly under a stained, floppy-brimmed hat. A large nose and a prominent jaw vied for her most noticeable feature. She looked up at Slocum with a drunken sneer as he went past.

"What can I do for you, gents?" asked the man behind the bar as Slocum and Delaney came up.

"If you've got a barrel of who-hit-John without too many rattlesnake heads floating in it, we'll take a couple of drinks," replied Slocum.

The man laughed. "No rattlesnake heads in my whiskey. I won't promise that there's not a little bit of black powder in it, though."

"Black powder never hurt anybody except when it was used to fire a bullet," Slocum said with a grin. This man was probably the proprietor of the trading post, and it wouldn't hurt anything to get on his good side right from the first. Slocum took the shot glass full of cloudy amber liquid that the bartender placed in front of him and tossed it back. The stuff burned like blazes all the way down his gullet and landed in his belly like a lead weight, but he just nodded appreciatively, set the glass down, and wiped the back of his left hand across his mouth.

"Smoothest you'll find between Fort Worth and El Paso," the bartender said proudly. Unfortunately, thought Slocum, that claim might well be truthful.

Delaney couldn't repress a shudder as he downed his drink, but the man behind the bar didn't appear to notice. Slocum said, "Are you the owner of this place?"

"That's me. W. H. Snyder. Call me Pete."

"Glad to meet you, Pete." Slocum took a coin from his pocket and laid it on the plank bar. The coin was enough to pay for the drinks several times over. "We're in the market for something else too."

"Better not be a woman," Snyder said with a grin. "Only one around here is Lucinda over there." He nodded toward the table where the woman Slocum had mistaken for a male buffalo hunter was sitting.

Slocum turned his head and smiled toward the table. "That's a pretty name," he said, loud enough for the woman to hear.

She cackled. "Go eat buffler shit, cowboy!" she called to him. "The likes o' you ain't gettin' none o' me."

The man at the table glowered at Slocum and Delaney and said, "If'n they want you, they got to wait in line like the rest of us, 'Cinda."

Slocum turned back to Snyder and said, "Truth is, we *are*

looking for a woman, Pete. A young blond woman who's got a baby with her.''

Without hesitation, Snyder gave an emphatic nod. ''She was here a couple of days ago. Didn't stay long—''

He didn't get a chance to finish what he was saying, because one of the men standing at the bar hawked loudly and spat on the floor. ''That *bitch*!'' he bellowed.

Delaney stiffened and turned sharply toward the man. ''What did you say?'' he demanded.

''I said that woman was a bitch!'' The man's natural tone of voice seemed to be a dull roar. ''That whore said she'd gimme some o' her sweetmeats, but she never did no such thing. She took off for the gap 'fore I got any lovin'. An' after I paid her an' all!''

''She's not a whore,'' Delaney said tightly, ignoring Slocum's warning frown.

Another man gave a raucous laugh. ''Hell, she could'a fooled me. I'd'a swore I give her four bits 'fore she let me hump her.''

''That's a damned lie!'' Delaney rapped out.

A strained silence fell over the trading post. It was broken when Snyder muttered under his breath, ''Oh, hell.''

''She's not a whore,'' Delaney said again as he glared at the men along the bar.

Lucinda spoke up from the table. ''That ain't what I heard. Shoot, after listenin' to these ol' boys talk about her, if I'd been here when that gal was, I might'a paid her four bits and taken a crack at her myself!''

Delaney spun toward her and snapped, ''Shut your mouth, you ugly old cow!''

Lucinda's eyes widened, and she slapped her callused palms down on the table. ''You little piss-ant!'' she shouted as she pushed herself unsteadily to her feet. ''You can't talk to a lady that way!''

She lunged at him, fists flailing.

Slocum had seen this mess coming, but there hadn't been much he could have done to stop it, short of clouting Delaney over the head and dragging him out of the trading post. He was starting to wish he had done just that.

Leaving Delaney to deal with Lucinda as best he could, Slocum pivoted toward the other men. They were taking Lucinda's side in this fracas, as Slocum had expected they would. Several of them had already clenched their fists and taken a couple of steps toward the two strangers at the bar.

Slocum's hand swept smoothly across his body toward the Colt. He palmed out the revolver in a motion that was almost too quick for the eye to follow. Before the hide hunters could move any closer, Slocum had the Colt up and leveled, his thumb looped over the hammer. He could empty the gun in a matter of seconds if he had to, and the ease and speed with which he had drawn it was enough to tell the men in the trading post that they had almost made a fatal mistake.

"Stay back, boys," Slocum said quietly. "This is none of your business."

"John, help!" Delaney bleated behind him. The cry was followed by a crash.

Slocum risked a glance over his shoulder, and saw that Delaney hadn't been able to fend off Lucinda's charge. She was taller and heavier than the pilgrim from St. Louis, and she had picked him up and slammed him against the bar. Instinctively, Slocum turned in that direction, knowing that if he didn't interfere, Lucinda was liable to beat Delaney to death.

That was a mistake. One of the hide hunters yelled, "Get him!" and something cracked across the wrist of the hand holding the Colt Navy.

Slocum grimaced as the gun flew out of his fingers. His hand had gone numb, and pain raced all the way up his arm to his shoulder. The man who had just hit him with an empty whiskey bottle was swinging the makeshift club back for another blow, this time undoubtedly to be aimed at Slocum's head. Slocum stepped closer to the man and swung his left fist, burying it in the hide hunter's belly.

He never should have come to the Panhandle, he realized now. He had been having trouble with these damned buffalo hunters ever since he'd set foot in Texas this time.

The man Slocum punched staggered back a step, gasping for breath. He blocked the others from getting at Slocum right away, giving the drifter a chance to try to pick up his fallen Colt. He lunged for the gun, which lay on the floor several feet away, reaching out with his left hand. He could handle the gun well enough with that hand to keep these drunken hunters back.

But he never got the chance to grab the Colt, because one of the men lashed out with a foot and kicked him in the side. Slocum was knocked away from the gun. He sprawled on the floor, and as he rolled over, he saw Delaney struggling futilely with Lucinda. In the glimpse he caught of their battle, he saw Lucinda bring her closed fist up and around in a pinwheeling blow that landed on top of Delaney's head. Delaney's derby had already fallen off, so there was nothing to cushion the impact. His eyes rolled up in his head.

Slocum didn't have time to see anything else, because the other hunters were rushing toward him, clearly intending to stomp him into the floor until there was nothing left but an ugly red paste. When the first man came within range, Slocum did some kicking of his own, driving the heel of his boot into the man's groin. The hunter shrieked and doubled over, crashing to the floor next to Slocum. Slocum rolled away and lunged up on his hands and knees. He tried to climb upright, and made it all the way to his feet before fists slammed into him and drove him back against the bar. One of the whiskey barrels overturned as Snyder let out an angry, frightened yell, and the whole bar collapsed. The barrel burst, and Slocum found himself awash in cheap whiskey and splintered wood. Fists were still coming at him, so he blocked all of them he could and set his feet to start throwing some punches of his own.

He didn't get to, because something hit him in the back of the head. He felt himself falling forward and tried to catch his balance, but the whole world seemed to be tilting crazily. Landing face-first in the spilled whiskey, he found himself blinded as the stuff splashed in his eyes and nose and mouth. He gasped for air, but just got more rotgut.

This was going to be one hell of a stupid way to die, he thought fleetingly, drowning facedown in a puddle of whiskey. He had always thought somehow that when his time came, he would go out on his feet, guns blazing. That was what he halfway hoped for, because the idea of dying in bed as a sick old man didn't appeal to him at all.

But that was life, he told himself. Ludicrous and humiliating and so damned unexpected, right to the end. . . .

The whiskey-reeking darkness claimed him.

16

And spat him back out, an unknown amount of time later. Slocum groaned, a little surprised that he was still alive. He had no doubt that he wasn't dead, because a dead man wouldn't be hurting as much as he was. Pain knifed through his head as he tried to move it, and his aching muscles refused to move as he attempted to push himself upright.

He was lying on his back. The smell of spilled whiskey was still quite strong in his nostrils. There was a yellow light to his left, so bright it hurt his eyes when he tried to look in that direction. He winced, and that made fresh waves of pain roll through his skull. Slowly, his vision cleared a little, and he could tell that the source of the light was one of the kerosene lanterns he had seen hanging in the trading post earlier, before the fight broke out.

That made him think about Delaney. Was Delaney still alive, or had Lucinda and the other buffalo hunters beaten him to death? That was what Slocum had expected to happen to *him* when he lost consciousness. He didn't think Delaney would have fared any better.

But he was alive, not dead, he reminded himself. If he had survived this ordeal, maybe Delaney had too.

Something moved between Slocum and the light. He tried to focus on it, but at first he could only see a looming black shape. A voice growled, "Wakin' up, are you, you son of a bitch?"

The voice was familiar, but it took Slocum a moment to place it. When he did, the knowledge didn't make him feel any better about his situation.

Mace Jones was standing over him.

Slocum's eyes had adjusted to the light well enough so that he could make out the buffalo hunter's features now. Mace had shed his buffalo-hide coat, and Slocum could see the bandages stained with old, dried blood that were wrapped around Mace's right arm and his side. Obviously, those bullets he had taken when he and his friends ambushed Slocum and Delaney hadn't killed him.

"I'd like to put my boot in your throat and push," Mace said with a sneer. "I'd pop your eyes outta your head just like they was grapes."

"Back off, Jones," said another voice. Slocum thought he had heard it before too, but he had even more trouble recognizing it than he had with Mace's voice. He still hadn't figured out who it belonged to by the time the man spoke again. "We didn't go to the trouble of saving these two from that bunch only to have you kill Slocum before we talk to him."

"I thought you wanted him dead," protested Mace.

"Not until I find out what I want to know."

Those words jogged Slocum's memory even more. The pain in his skull had receded a little, so he tried turning his head. He was able to this time, and what he saw came as no real surprise.

The big man standing on Slocum's other side opposite from Mace Jones was still wearing the duster and the flat-crowned hat. He looked the same as he had back in Tascosa, when he had busted into Lady Arabella Winthrop's room and threatened to kill her if Slocum didn't tell him about a baby.

"Is your name . . . Kelso?" Slocum croaked, forcing the words out past a throat sore from being punched or kicked in the melee.

That surprised the man in the duster. He blinked, then

frowned down at Slocum and asked, "How the hell did you know that?"

With an effort, Slocum lifted his right arm. "Get me . . . up," he said, ignoring the question.

Kelso's frown deepened, but he leaned over and clasped Slocum's wrist. Slocum grabbed hold and hung on as Kelso hauled him into a sitting position. From there, Slocum was able to look around and see that he was still inside Snyder's Trading Post, just as he had thought. Snyder himself was sitting at the table where Lucinda had been earlier, his head in his hands, obviously discouraged over the damage that had been done to his establishment. Calvin Delaney was slumped over another table, either unconscious or dead. A shuddering moan that came from the pilgrim told Slocum it was the former. There was no sign of the buffalo hunters who had started the fight.

"Get him on his feet," Kelso said curtly to Mace, pointing at Slocum with a thumb as he did so.

"Do it yourself," snapped Mace. "This hole in my side is still healin'."

A humorless grin stretched Kelso's mouth. "Sounds like you've forgotten who saved your life, Mace. Reckon it's mine to take away just as easy."

Mace glowered and muttered, but he stepped over behind Slocum and reached down to hook his hands under Slocum's arms. Slocum tried to brace himself, but he was too late. Mace jerked him roughly to his feet, making more pain shoot through Slocum's head and body.

It would have been easy to let himself pass out again. Instead, Slocum's brain started working. He tried to concentrate on the dilemma facing him, rather than the fact that he hurt like hell. He wasn't sure how Mace and Kelso had gotten hooked up together, but that didn't really matter. What was important was that both of them wanted him dead, only Kelso didn't want to see that happen right away. He wanted information first—before he put a bullet in Slocum's head.

Which meant that the worst thing Slocum could do would

be to tell Kelso that he was looking for the wrong baby. Slocum had come damn close to blurting out that Kelso was on the wrong trail, that the baby Slocum and Delaney sought was little Edgar, not the kidnapped Kenneth Mulwray. Once Kelso was convinced of that, he wouldn't have any reason for keeping Slocum alive. He could turn Slocum over to Mace and ride away.

But Slocum had already revealed that he knew Kelso's name, which had made the detective mighty curious. Kelso caught hold of Slocum's arm and marched him over to a vacant table. "Sit down," he growled. "I'll get you a drink."

Slocum shook his head slowly. The stink of the rotgut whiskey that had soaked into his clothes left him with no desire for a drink.

"All right," Kelso said. He pulled out a chair and sat down on the other side of the table. "Then start talking. Tell me what I want to know."

"Tell me what happened here first," rasped Slocum. "What happened to those buffalo hunters?"

"They decided to leave." Kelso moved aside the left-hand flap of his duster to reveal a sawed-off shotgun hanging under his left arm in a specially made holster. "Stomping you to death would have been fun, but not worth their lives."

"So you came in just in time to run them off before they killed Delaney and me."

Kelso nodded. "That's right. So you owe your life to me too, Slocum, just like Mace here." That comment brought another glare from Mace. Kelso ignored him and went on. "I can't have you dying until you tell me all you know about that missing baby."

Movement caught Slocum's eye. He looked past Kelso and saw Delaney lifting his head from the other table. There was a dazed look on Delaney's face, which was bruised and swollen and scraped raw in places. Slocum figured he looked just as bad or worse. Kelso's questions about a baby had caught Delaney's attention, penetrating the fog in his brain. Slocum knew he had to act quickly to keep Delaney from ruining everything.

Memories of the conversations he'd had with Sheila Mulwray gave him the clue he needed in order to decide on a course of action. He laughed harshly and said, "You're not the only one looking for the Mulwray kid, Kelso. My partner and I figure there'll be a big payoff for us if we're the ones to find that baby."

He spoke loudly enough so that Delaney could hear him clearly. Delaney turned bleary eyes toward him, and the question remained whether or not he understood what Slocum was trying to do. Slocum could only hope that he did.

"Son of a bitch," said Kelso, but it was a curse, not an insult directed at Slocum. "I was afraid of that. It's not enough that Mulwray hired me *and* the Pinkertons to look for the kid. Him and that round-heeled wife of his have been telling everybody they meet about the kidnapping ever since they left Chicago." He drew his gun and laid it meaningfully on the table in front of him. "So you're looking for the baby on your own, and if you find him, you expect a big reward from the Mulwrays."

Somehow, Slocum managed to give a grim chuckle. "Hell, it's not worth getting killed over. We didn't know we were crossing over into your territory, Kelso. Did we, Delaney?"

Slocum waited anxiously. He wasn't sure if Delaney had even understood the question. But after a couple of seconds, the pilgrim shook his head and said through thick lips, "Sorry, mister. We'll back off."

So Delaney had been quick enough on the uptake after all. Slocum felt a surge of relief. Of course, there was still Mace Jones to deal with. . . .

"He don't know anything," Mace said. "Let's kill him now."

Slocum glared up at the buffalo hunter. "You took that shot at me from the alley in Tascosa, didn't you?"

"And I'd'a killed you then and there too if you weren't so damned lucky." Mace reached for the Bowie knife sheathed at his hip. "I think I'll carve my name in your hide before I kill you, Slocum."

Slocum looked at Kelso. "You let him kill me, and you're liable to lose out on something you want to know."

"Like what?" asked Kelso.

"Maybe I know where that kid is." It was a bold lie that Slocum was implying, but he didn't have any options left except bold ones.

"If he knows, that partner of his knows too," Mace put in. "So let's go ahead and kill Slocum—"

"Shut up, Mace! I swear, you make it hard for a man to think." Kelso regarded Slocum coolly. "You could be lying just to save your hide," he said.

"I could be," Slocum agreed, "or I could be telling the truth." He shrugged. "You'll have to decide."

Slocum leaned back in his chair, infinitely tired. The long chase, the attempts on his life, the passionate interludes with Arabella and Sheila, the fight here at Snyder's . . . all of these had combined to produce a weariness of mind and body and soul. But despite that, Slocum's thoughts were still whirling as he waited for Kelso to decide what to do next. The desperate gamble Slocum was taking depended on him being able to remember what one of those buffalo hunters had said about Rose just before the fracas broke out.

She took off for the gap. Those were the words Slocum had been trying to recall. He remembered as well what Molly Goodnight had said about the settlements in this area. The next one of any size was called Buffalo Gap. That had to have been Rose's destination. At the very least, she had been heading in that direction when she left Snyder.

If he could convince Kelso that he really had a lead on the missing Mulwray baby, he might be able to talk the gunman into sparing his life and Delaney's. Slocum was going to propose a partnership of sorts: Kelso could ride with them, but Slocum wouldn't tell him where they were going until they got there. That way Slocum and Delaney could not only stay alive, but they might wind up finding Rose and Edgar. Of course, that wouldn't help Kenneth Mulwray, but there were plenty of other detectives already searching for the kidnapped boy. At the moment, Slocum was more concerned with saving his hide and catching up to Rose.

Sorting out all these possibilities and muddled motivations was damned hard on the brain, thought Slocum. He wished he could just shoot somebody and be done with it.

"He's lyin', I tell you—" Mace began.

"Shut up," said Kelso. "I'm tired of telling you that I'll do the thinking, Mace. If you don't like it, you can ride out any time you want."

Mace clenched his fists. "Maybe I'll just do that," he blustered. "I don't need you, mister. I can take care of myself." He glanced at Slocum. "And I can settle my own debts too."

Kelso snorted in contempt. "You weren't good enough to kill Slocum and this other fella when you and your friends had them outnumbered two to one. You really think you can go up against all three of us, Mace, and live to tell about it?"

All three of us. Slocum liked the sound of that. It meant Kelso had taken the bait, or was at least nibbling mighty eagerly on it.

Mace was red-faced with frustration under his whiskers. He looked fit to bust, Slocum thought. But despite his hunger for vengeance, Mace was no fool. He knew that there had been a realignment of alliances here, taking place so subtly that he had almost missed it. If he tried to kill Slocum now, it would just backfire on him, most likely in fatal fashion.

After a minute, Mace said, *"Shit!"* between clenched teeth. That just about summed it up, Slocum thought. Mace turned and stalked toward the door of the trading post. He slapped it open and stepped out into the dusk. The door slammed behind him.

"We'll stay here tonight," Kelso announced. He looked over at Pete Snyder, who was taking more of an interest in the conversation now that Mace was gone. "You've got some rooms we can rent, don't you, mister?"

Snyder shook his head. "Nope, 'fraid not. But you're welcome to stay out in the barn if you'd like. After everything that's happened, I wouldn't charge you.''

Kelso stood up and brought a coin from his vest pocket. He tossed it onto the other table and said, "We'll pay. There's enough there to cover that busted barrel and the whiskey you lost too."

Snyder scooped up the money. "I . . . I'm much obliged, mister."

Kelso looked down at Slocum. "Don't get any funny ideas," he warned. "You try any tricks and I'll kill you and your partner—what's his name, Delaney?—faster than you can blink. I'm not completely convinced you know anything about that missing kid anyway."

Coolly, Slocum returned the gunman's stare. "I reckon we'll just have to wait and see who's telling the truth, won't we?"

"And who lives and who dies," Kelso added with a grin.

17

Luck was with them. Kelso hadn't talked to any of the buffalo
hunters who had been hanging around Snyder's before the
fight, or he might have found out the same thing Slocum had,
namely that a woman with a baby had come through the settlement and left headed toward Buffalo Gap. Since Kelso had
threatened them with their lives when he broke up the fracas,
none of the hunters returned to the trading post that night. Nor
did Mace Jones. So the next morning, bright and early, Slocum
and Delaney were able to leave town with Kelso riding alongside them. The gunman didn't trust them for a second—and
the feeling was mutual, of course—but he was willing to play
along in hopes of finding the Mulwray baby.

Kelso had bedded down in the barn with them, and had
been within earshot all night, so Slocum hadn't had a chance
to discuss the situation with Delaney. So far, Delaney had
seemed to understand what Slocum was trying to do. Slocum
could only hope that continued.

"Better keep your eyes open," Slocum commented as they
rode out of the settlement. "Mace is liable to try to bushwhack
all three of us."

Kelso nodded. "I don't reckon he'd draw the line at back-
shooting."

"What about you?"

141

That ugly grin stretched across Kelso's face again. "I never shot a man in the back . . . unless he happened to be turned that way."

Slocum and Delaney exchanged a grim glance. Neither of them doubted that Kelso was telling the truth.

This was flat country, dotted with clumps of brush and groves of stubby trees. Small creeks cut through it in places, but they were narrow and shallow and easy to cross. In the distance, mesas and ranges of hills were visible from time to time, but the route followed by Slocum and his two companions was pretty monotonous. That was the way Slocum liked it. Easy terrain like this meant there weren't as many places where an ambusher—such as Mace Jones—could hide.

Slocum decided he might as well do a little probing while they rode. He said to Kelso, "How'd you wind up being a detective? You don't seem much like a Pinkerton to me."

"I'm not a damned Pink," said Kelso. "I rode for that damned strait-laced Scotsman for a while, but he and I never did see eye to eye about anything. Did some work for the railroads, then hired on as town marshal up in Nebraska. Didn't like that either. So I decided I could do anything the Pinks can and went into business for myself. I don't like to have anybody riding me. I work my own way, and I get results."

What Kelso meant, thought Slocum, was that he didn't like having somebody looking over his shoulder while he murdered and threatened people to find out what he wanted to know. Slocum could understand why Kelso hadn't like working for Allen Pinkerton. The Pinkerton agents had a reputation for playing rough sometimes, but they weren't out-and-out killers. Kelso didn't have a hint of true human feelings inside him. Those pale blue eyes of his reminded Slocum of a snake's eyes.

Slocum figured they could make the ride from Snyder to Buffalo Gap in two, maybe two and a half days if they didn't run into any trouble. He hoped that Rose would stay put this time when she reached the settlement. She had been moving steadily for a couple of weeks now, and she and Edgar had to be getting worn out. Where was she headed anyway? Or did she even have some destination in mind?

Maybe she was just running, he thought. He glanced over at Delaney as they rode. Maybe Rose just wanted to get as far away from her husband as she possibly could.

After a period of silence, Kelso abruptly asked, "Who's the woman?"

"What?" Slocum said.

"The woman who has the baby now. You were asking questions about a pretty young blond woman in Tascosa. Who is she? The Mulwray kid was snatched by two men in Chicago."

Slocum shrugged. "How the hell would I know? Maybe she's somebody the kidnappers hired to look after the baby. *I* wouldn't want to have to take care of a kid like that." He spun out the yarn a little farther, using his imagination. "Or maybe *she* stole the kid from the gents who took him from his aunt and uncle. All I know is that she's got him."

"And we're on her trail now," Kelso said heavily.

"We're on her trail now," Slocum said with a confident nod.

"I guess we can figure it all out once we've got the kid."

"Yeah, sure." What Kelso meant was that once Kenneth Mulwray had been rescued, he could kill Slocum and Delaney and rid himself of an inconvenience. Slocum had no doubt that was what Kelso was planning.

But it wasn't going to work out that way. Slocum was going to see to that.

He and Kelso checked their back trail frequently. Between the two of them, Slocum thought, it was unlikely Mace would be able to follow them without being seen. Maybe the vengeful buffalo hunter had finally given up. Slocum hoped that was the case, but he wasn't going to hold his breath waiting for Mace to see the light of reason.

On the second day, the terrain became more rugged and the live oak thickets more common. By noon, Slocum could see

a range of hills in the distance to the southeast, with a prominent notch in the center of them. "That's the Callahan Divide," he said as he nodded toward the hills, searching his
memory for their name.

"Is that where we're going?" Kelso asked.

Slocum shrugged. "Could be."

"You're a close-mouthed bastard. Normally I don't like that
in a man. I reckon you've got your reasons, though."

And they both knew what those reasons were, thought Slocum. The information he claimed to have was the only thing
keeping Kelso from trying to kill him.

"You'd better not be stringing me along," Kelso added, as
if he had been reading Slocum's mind. "I wouldn't take
kindly to that."

"You'll see," Slocum said. "When we get where we're
going, the woman and the baby will be there." He just didn't
explain which woman and baby he was talking about.

By the time dusk was settling down, the three riders could
see the lights of a settlement twinkling in the distance. The
lights were located in that notch in the hills, and Slocum knew
they had to mark the site of Buffalo Gap. It was easy to see
why the town had gotten its name. The vast herds of shaggy
beasts that had roamed these plains for centuries would have
beaten a natural path through that gap in their annual migra-
tions. It was the easiest way through the Callahan Divide.

"Is that where we're going?" growled Kelso.

"Could be," Slocum replied. "Or maybe it's just another
stop along the trail. Either way, it makes sense to push on and
spend the night there, rather than camping out here."

Kelso nodded in agreement. "I've always liked sleeping in
a bed better than on the ground."

Since leaving the farm in Georgia to go off to war, Slocum
had probably spent more nights under the stars than he had
with a roof over his head. As long as the weather wasn't too
bad, it didn't matter much to him either way. But he was glad
Kelso wasn't going to balk at going into the settlement.

Night had fallen when they rode in. The dwellings and businesses of Buffalo Gap were arranged around a rough square with a solid-looking rock structure in the center of it. A couple of windows were lit in the building, and Slocum could see the iron bars across those windows. A cold finger touched his spine. He didn't like jails, never had. But he didn't have any reason to fear this one. He didn't aim to do anything that would land him there.

The three men steered their horses toward a saloon. As they rode past the other buildings, Slocum saw a general store, a blacksmith shop, a saddle maker's establishment, a doctor's office, and even a bank, in addition to a dozen or more houses. Buffalo Gap was a substantial little town for a frontier settlement, though it looked pretty sleepy at the moment. Just out of professional curiosity, he wondered how much cash there was inside the stone walls of that bank, then gave a little shake of his head and put that thought out of his mind. He was here to find Rose and Edgar, not to rob a bank.

"All right, Slocum," Kelso said in a low, dangerous voice as they reined to a halt in front of the saloon. "Time for you to start telling the truth. Are we going to find that woman and kid here or not?"

"You want the truth, I'll give it to you. I don't know if they're here. But they were headed in this direction."

Kelso glared at him for a second, then said, "You've got balls, you know that? You told me you knew where the baby was just so I wouldn't kill you."

"I'd've been a damned fool to admit that I didn't know for sure, wouldn't I?" replied Slocum. "But if you want to do something about it, Kelso, go ahead and make your move." Slocum was tired of playing games. If Kelso wanted to try to take him, the gunman was welcome to make a stab at it. Slocum would match his own speed and accuracy against Kelso's, and let the best man win.

Kelso grunted and swung down off his horse. "Come on," he said. "Let's go see what we can find out."

Slocum let out a breath he hadn't even been aware he was

holding. Obviously, Kelso was willing to let their reluctant partnership continue for the time being.

"I thought he was going to kill you," Delaney said in a half whisper.

"I thought maybe he was going to try," Slocum said. He dismounted, tied his horse to the hitch rack in front of the saloon, and followed Kelso onto the low porch of the establishment. Delaney brought up the rear.

The doors of the saloon were closed against the chill of the night. Slocum, Kelso, and Delaney went inside and found themselves in a long, narrow room with a hardwood bar running along the left-hand wall, complete with a brass rail along the bottom. There were booths on the right wall and tables in the center of the room, which was lit by a couple of chandeliers. This was a lot fancier place than Snyder's Trading Post had been, but it wasn't any busier this evening. In fact, there were only four men in the saloon, three standing in front of the bar, one behind it. They all turned to look curiously at Slocum, Kelso, and Delaney.

"Evenin', gents," called the man behind the bar, who was short, balding, and moon-faced. "What's your poison?"

"Beer," said Slocum as he came up to the bar. Both Kelso and Delaney nodded in agreement, and the bartender began drawing three beers. Slocum glanced at the other customers. One of them had the look of a successful cattleman, while the other two were townsmen. They nodded politely to Slocum.

"Howdy," said the rancher in friendly tones. "Just get into town?"

"That's right," Slocum replied. He had assumed the role of spokesman. "Just rode in from Snyder."

"You mean that place ain't dried up and blowed away yet?" asked one of the townies. The question brought a chuckle from his companions.

"No, it's still there," Slocum said. "Reckon it will be as long as the buffalo hold out."

The cattleman said, "That won't be too much longer, I hope. This settlement got its name from them, but we never see them around here anymore. Good riddance, I say. It's a waste of good grazing land to have all those buffalo taking it up.''

Slocum's jaw tightened, but he managed not to spit out the retort that wanted to come to his lips. All the wild places of the West would be tamed soon enough, he thought. He sure as hell wasn't going to wish that civilization would hurry up and wipe out all the vestiges of what the frontier had once been.

He didn't want to anger these men, so he just grunted non-committally and then said, ''Buy you boys a drink?''

''Sure,'' piped up the other townie. He wasn't just about to turn down a free drink, and neither were his two companions. Slocum looked meaningfully at Kelso, and the detective dug out a coin that he dropped on the bar. The bartender made it disappear and drew beers for the cattleman and the two townies.

''We're looking for somebody,'' Kelso said bluntly after the men had sipped from their mugs of beer. ''A woman traveling with a baby.''

Slocum might not have been so straightforward about what they wanted to buy with those beers, but maybe Kelso had a point, he thought. Maybe enough time had been wasted.

The rancher frowned. ''A woman traveling alone except for a child? We don't see such things much in this part of the country. Don't see all that many women, to tell you the truth. There's not more than half a dozen in town, and they've all been here for a spell.''

''Then you haven't seen her?'' asked Slocum, willing to follow Kelso's lead for the time being.

''Nope.''

''That's because you're not always here in town, Chet,'' one of the townies said. ''Alvin and I saw her, didn't we?'' He turned to the other townsman for confirmation.

Alvin grinned. ''Young and blond and pretty? That the one you're looking for?''

''That's right,'' Slocum said, feeling himself tense. Beside him, Kelso and Delaney were reacting the same way.

"Yeah, we saw her a couple of days ago," Alvin said. "She came into my store to get some canned milk for the baby. But she didn't have any money."

Delaney said, "You gave her the milk anyway, didn't you?"

Alvin smirked. "She got the milk, but I didn't give it to her. We came to an agreement. Jed was there too, so since he's my friend, I said she'd have to do us both before I'd let her have any supplies."

Jed slapped Alvin on the shoulder. "And I can't thank you enough for including me, pard. That gal was the best I'd had in a long time—"

Slocum had glanced over at Delaney a second earlier and seen how the man had gone pale. He had noted the sudden tremble in Delaney's muscles. So he was ready when Delaney made his move—or at least he thought he was. But Delaney acted faster than Slocum had expected. The pilgrim lunged past Slocum and crashed into Jed, fastening his hands around the townie's neck. "Shut up!" Delaney howled. "Shut your lying mouth!" Both men went down, sprawling on the floor.

"Hey!" yelled Alvin. He and the rancher, Chet, reached for Delaney and pulled him off their friend. They flung him against the bar. Delaney slammed into the hardwood with what had to be a bone-numbing impact. Alvin and Chet grabbed him again as he bounced off the bar.

Jed was scrambling to his feet. "Hang on to that son of a bitch!" he yelled. "I'll teach him a lesson."

Slocum and Kelso had had enough of this. They palmed out their guns at the same instant, and Slocum said in a quiet, menacing tone, "Hold it. That's enough."

Jed, Alvin, and Chet froze. The man behind the bar was equally motionless as he stared at the guns in the hands of Slocum and Kelso.

Then Kelso took a step back and pivoted slightly, so that

the muzzle of the Colt in his hand was pressed to Slocum's head, just behind Slocum's right ear. ''That's enough, all right,'' Kelso said. ''You've been lying to me all along, Slocum. Now I want the truth.''

18

Shit, thought Slocum. Kelso had figured it out. He had hoped that the implications of Delaney's sudden assault on Jed would escape the gunman's notice.

But they hadn't, and now he wasn't going to be able to bluff his way out of this. But he supposed he would have to try anyway. There was nothing else he could do—except tell the truth.

"What the hell are you talking about, Kelso?" he demanded roughly. "I thought we were partners, damn it!"

"You thought wrong," Kelso said, his voice as cold as his eyes always were. "I let you and Delaney live because I thought you might lead me to that baby. Now I see it's all been a wild-goose chase."

"What makes you say that?"

"You claimed you and Delaney were trying to find the kid so you could claim a reward from the Mulwrays. But Delaney knows that woman, doesn't he? You've been playing me for a fool. You've been part of it all along." Kelso prodded Slocum's skull painfully with the barrel of his gun. "The two of you kidnapped the Mulwray brat in the first place, didn't you? Then you either brought the woman in on the plan, or she was part of it from the first. Either way, she double-crossed you by taking off with the kid. I should have seen that right away,

150

but I never tumbled to it until just now, when I realized that Delaney already knows the woman we're after.''

Well, son of a bitch, Slocum thought. Kelso hadn't guessed the truth after all. The detective had come up with yet another explanation that made sense, despite the fact that it was completely wrong.

Chet said, ''Uh, mister . . . you want to put that gun down?'' The rancher's face was covered with beads of sweat. Jed and Alvin looked just as nervous. Slocum's Colt Navy was still pointing at them, even though they had released Delaney and moved a step away from him. The hammer of the gun was eared back, and if Slocum let it fall for any reason—such as Kelso shooting him—the Colt would go off. Under the circumstances, Slocum couldn't blame them for being a mite skittish.

''Look, Kelso, we'd better talk about this,'' Slocum began.

''Nothing to talk about. You tell me the truth and maybe I don't kill you. Stall, or lie to me, and you die right here and now, Slocum.''

Delaney was leaning on the bar, winded from the heavy impact of being thrown against it. Between gasps for breath, he looked up at Jed and Alvin and said, ''You . . . you can't talk about . . . my wife like that.''

''Thanks, Delaney,'' Kelso said dryly. ''You just admitted I was right about part of it anyway. How about it, Slocum? You going to tell me the rest, or am I going to blow your damned head off and be done with it?''

''All right,'' Slocum said wearily. ''We kidnapped the kid. I don't know why Rose ran out with him, but she did.''

Delaney blinked several times, clearly struggling to follow what Slocum was saying. The bartender and the saloon's three customers were looking more nervous all the time. Guns being waved around, kidnappings, double crosses . . . this was more than they had bargained for when they stopped in for a friendly drink.

''Where is she now?'' Kelso grated.

''I don't know,'' Slocum replied, and it felt a little strange to be telling the truth for once. He waggled the barrel of his gun at Jed and Alvin. "Ask these hombres. They seem to know as much as Delaney and I do. They've seen her since we have."

"We didn't do anything to the woman!" Jed burst out. "Alvin was lying. We saw her in his store, but we didn't do anything, I swear it!"

"That's right," added Alvin. "I . . . I got a wife and kids. I wouldn't do anything like that. But she was really pretty and I . . . we . . . it was just bragging, you know?"

Delaney glared at them. "You sons of bitches. You never even thought about the fact you were spreading rumors about a married woman, did you?"

Kelso said, "I don't give a damn about the woman's reputation. I just want to know where she went."

"Cross Plains," Jed answered without hesitation. "That's where she told us she was going. Said she had family there."

Alvin nodded emphatically. "That's right. She said she was headed for Cross Plains."

"Where's that?" asked Kelso.

"It's a little settlement 'bout fifty miles southeast of here," replied Chet. "A stagecoach road and a trail laid out by the army meet up there, on a little stream called Turkey Creek. Bunch of Dutchmen settled there first, called the place Schleicher. They changed the name to Cross Plains earlier this year when they got their own post office. I got a cousin lives there."

That was more information than Kelso really wanted. "Stop babbling," he snapped at the rancher. "I reckon that's all I need to know. Drop your gun, Slocum."

"Don't believe I will," Slocum replied coolly. "If you gun me, then Delaney will get you and you'll never see that reward the Mulwrays promised you."

Kelso laughed harshly and disdainfully. "That pilgrim's going to drop me? Hell, Slocum, I could put a bullet through your head and shoot him three times before he even got his gun out."

"You willing to risk your life on that? I saw Delaney take down two of those buffalo hunters who jumped us with Mace Jones. He killed them just as cool as you please, a bullet in the head for each one of them." Of course, that had been blind luck, thought Slocum, but there was no need for Kelso to know that. And the fact of the matter was, Delaney *had* killed those buffalo hunters.

Slocum sensed Kelso's hesitation. The detective blustered, "Maybe so, but you'd still be dead."

Slocum's shoulders rose and fell slightly in a minuscule shrug. "So would you."

Before Kelso could make up his mind one way or the other, a new voice came from an open doorway at the end of the bar. "You boys stand easy," it said firmly. "Chet, Jed, Alvin, get out of the damn way!"

The locals scattered, obviously familiar with the owner of the voice. Slocum and Kelso found themselves facing a man on the far side of middle age. He had white hair and a handlebar mustache, and a shotgun was gripped tightly in his big, callused hands. A tin star was pinned to his coat.

"Sheriff Farnsworth," the bartender said, a sigh of relief in his voice. "How did you—"

"Saw what was goin' on through the window," the lawman said. "So I snuck around and came in your back door."

Delaney looked back over his shoulder at the sheriff. Farnsworth went on. "Just you be careful, young fella. If I have to squeeze these triggers, a good chunk of this charge of buckshot's goin' to hit you."

"They're kidnappers, Sheriff!" Jed said excitedly, raising a hand to point at Slocum and Delaney. "Those two right there. They admitted it. They stole a baby, and the other fella's hunting it!"

Farnsworth's eyes narrowed. "Stole a baby from its folks? That's just about the lowest thing I've ever heard."

The gun barrel went away from Slocum's head. "That's what I thought, Sheriff," Kelso said. "That's why I set out to track down the child and the bastards responsible for kidnapping him. My name's Kelso, and I'm a detective from Kansas City. I'm working for the baby's guardians.''

Well, this mess just kept finding new and unexpected ways to get worse, Slocum told himself.

Kelso stepped to the side, keeping his gun trained on Slocum but putting himself out of the line of fire of the lawman's greener. "We'd better throw these two in your jail.''

"I reckon you're right," Farnsworth agreed. To Slocum he said, "Put that gun on the bar right now, mister, or I'll be usin' this scattergun in about two shakes of a lamb's tail.''

Slocum grimaced, then let his breath out in a sigh. "All right, Sheriff," he said. He lowered the Colt, turned and placed it on the bar.

"Slide it down here to me," commanded Farnsworth. Slocum did as he was told. "Now your partner.''

"Do it," Slocum said to Delaney. There was a lost, defeated look in Delaney's eyes, and he complied without argument. When they were both disarmed, the sheriff stepped out from behind the end of the bar and came toward them, keeping the shotgun pointed at them.

"Before I go to lockin' folks up," he said to Kelso, "you got any bona fides to prove you're tellin' the truth?''

"Of course, Sheriff," Kelso replied with a confident grin. "I have my identification papers, as well as a letter from the guardians of the missing boy authorizing me to conduct a search for him and the men who kidnapped him. I'd be glad to show them to you.''

"Well, let's get these two rapscallions behind bars first," Farnsworth decided after a moment's thought. "Then I'll look at your papers.''

"As long as I'm not delayed for too great a period of time," said Kelso. "I know where the missing lad is now, and I want to get to him as soon as I can.''

"Sure thing." Farnsworth jerked the barrels of the greener toward the door of the saloon. "You two—*git*!''

There was nothing else they could do. With Farnsworth and

Kelso trailing them, Slocum and Delaney were marched to the sturdy stone jail in the center of Buffalo Gap's town square.

The clang of a cell door closing was one of the ugliest sounds in the world, Slocum had thought many times in the past. The one here in Buffalo Gap didn't sound any better as Sheriff Farnsworth shut it firmly and turned the key.

"There. You boys ain't goin' anywhere until we get to the bottom o' this." Farnsworth turned to Kelso, who stood in the doorway of the cell block. "Now let's go out in the office and have a look at them papers of yours."

Kelso and the lawman disappeared into the sheriff's office, leaving the heavy wooden cell block door open just slightly. Slocum and Delaney stood in the cell and exchanged a solemn glance. "What the hell do we do now?" asked Delaney. He sounded as if he wanted to groan in dismay.

"We wait until we get a chance to get out of here," Slocum said. He wrapped his fingers tightly around the bars of the cell door and tried to suppress the emotions raging inside him. He had never liked being locked up. And he was mad too: mad at Kelso for the most part, but also angry at the fates that had sent him on this long, winding trail in pursuit of Rose Delaney. He should have cut his losses and stayed in Tascosa. If he had done that, he would be in the Deuces right now, he thought, enjoying a poker game or a drink or the magnificent pleasures of Lady Arabella Winthrop's body. Instead, he was behind bars—again.

But this time there was no doubt he was innocent. He hadn't been anywhere within a thousand miles of Chicago when the Mulwray baby had been kidnapped. Given time, he could prove that.

Time was something he didn't have a lot of, not if he wanted to find Rose and Edgar. He didn't know whether to hope they had stayed in Cross Plains or not. If Rose had been telling the truth about having relatives there, her flight might have finally ended in the small settlement.

The same thing was obviously on Delaney's mind. He said,

"What's Kelso going to do when he finds Rose and the boy and realizes he's been tricked? He's liable to take it out on them."

"He's got more sense than that," Slocum said, hoping that he was right. "If he harms an innocent woman and child, there won't be any place in Texas he can hide from the folks who'll be after him."

Delaney snorted. "Kelso does what he wants. He's not going to worry about the law or anything else."

Slocum didn't say anything. He was trying to listen to what Kelso and Sheriff Farnsworth were saying in the office. He could make out their voices, but the words were muffled and difficult to distinguish.

After a few moments, though, Slocum heard the scrape of a chair. Then the sheriff's voice, pitched a little louder now, came plainly to his ears. "Everything looks to be in order, Mr. Kelso," said Farnsworth. "Reckon you can be ridin' on. I'll keep those two prisoners here and get in touch with the Rangers to come an' take charge of 'em."

"You do that, Sheriff," Kelso said. Slocum heard his footsteps as he turned and started to walk toward the outer door of the office.

"Wait just a minute!" Farnsworth's voice ripped out. "Hold on, Kelso. It's been botherin' me all evenin', thinkin' that I've seen you before. Now I believe I recollect where it was." Slocum tensed as he heard papers being shuffled. "Yeah, here it is!" exclaimed Farnsworth, excitement in his voice. "I got a reward dodger on you. You're wanted in Galveston for gunnin' a fella named Smith!"

"That's a mistake, Sheriff," snapped Kelso. "I've never even been to Galveston."

"Don't you take another step!" The metallic clicking of a pistol being cocked came from the office. "I reckon we'll have to let the Rangers hash *this* out too. You're goin' behind bars until they get here."

"You can't do that," Kelso said.

"Don't worry, I'll put you in a different cell from those

other two, so they won't bother you. Now take off that gunbelt and drop it on the floor . . . nice and easy, now.''

Delaney looked at Slocum and grinned. ''Kelso's getting his comeuppance after all,'' he said quietly.

Slocum wasn't so pleased with what he was hearing, even though if Kelso was locked up, he couldn't beat them to Rose and Edgar. But as Slocum heard the sound of Kelso's gunbelt hitting the floor and then Farnsworth ordered, ''Go on over to the cell block,'' a memory flashed vividly in Slocum's mind— a memory of the sawed-off shotgun hidden under Kelso's coat.

''Sheriff!'' Slocum yelled suddenly. ''Look out, he's got a—''

The dull boom of a shotgun shell exploding drowned out the rest of Slocum's warning.

19

With a heavy thud, Sheriff Farnsworth's body slammed into the cell block door and knocked it all the way open. The lawman pitched backward and landed on the stone floor of the cell block, his chest a bloody mess where the blast from Kelso's hidden shotgun had caught him. Farnsworth was still holding his six-gun in his hand, but as he landed it slipped from his fingers and went spinning across the floor toward the cells.

Without even thinking about what he was doing, Slocum dropped to his knees and lunged against the bars of the cell door, reaching through them desperately and stretching out his hand toward the spot where the sheriff's gun had come to rest.

Slocum's fingers closed around the walnut grips of Farnsworth's .45 as Kelso's big shape loomed in the cell block door. Instinct had told Slocum that after murdering the sheriff, Kelso wouldn't want to leave any witnesses behind. Only one barrel of that sawed-off had been discharged. The other one would be plenty to take care of Slocum and Delaney since there was nowhere to hide in the small cell.

But before Kelso could bring the weapon in his hands to bear, Slocum tipped up the sheriff's Colt and triggered a shot. The angle was bad and the gun unfamiliar to him, but Slocum put the bullet close to where he wanted it. The slug chewed splinters from the door jamb only inches from Kelso's head. Kelso jerked back involuntarily, and Slocum fired again. This time the shot whipped through the open doorway, and Slocum couldn't tell where it landed.

He heard the thud of Kelso's boots on the floor, though, as the killer fled. Kelso had to know the shots would bring the townspeople on the run, and he wanted to be away from the jail before he could be trapped here. He still had a baby to find and a reward to claim—or at least he thought so.

Kelso's decision to run had given Slocum and Delaney a reprieve, but only for the moment. They would still be in bad shape when the citizens got here and found their sheriff lying dead on the cell block floor. As admitted kidnappers, the two men would be prime suspects in Farnsworth's death, even though they were locked up and the sheriff had been killed with a shotgun. Those were details a lynch mob might not notice until *after* they had strung up a couple of innocent men.

"What are we going to do?" Delaney asked as Slocum got to his feet, still holding the sheriff's gun.

"We're going to get out of here," Slocum replied, "and it's got to be quick." He tucked the Colt behind his belt and went to the far corner of the cell, nearest to where Farnsworth's body lay. He could see the ring of keys still attached to the old lawman's belt. Once again Slocum knelt and reached through the bars.

Farnsworth's out-flung right hand was just tantalizingly out of reach. Slocum strained against the bars, trying to make his shoulder smaller so that it could slip a little farther between the bars and give him the couple of inches he needed. A ludicrous image suddenly passed through his mind: himself, stuck tight between the bars with a dead lawman only inches away. He grunted with effort as he tried to extend his reach.

His fingertips brushed the sleeve of the sheriff's coat.

Slocum scrabbled for a better hold, and after what seemed like forever was finally able to grasp Farnsworth's sleeve tightly enough to start hauling the corpse toward the cell. The sheriff's dead weight was considerable, and again Slocum grunted and groaned. Farnsworth's body slowly slid closer.

Delaney knelt beside Slocum and reached through the bars. "Let me help." He was able to catch hold and add his strength to Slocum's. Together, they pulled Farnsworth up against the bars. Slocum reached for the ring of keys and ripped them from the dead man's belt. He couldn't believe that none of the townspeople had gotten here yet. Retrieving the keys must not have taken as long as it seemed, he thought. He stood up, his arm and shoulder aching, and hurried to the cell door. It took several seconds to thrust the right key into the lock and turn it, but then he and Delaney were free and stepping out of the cell.

Now Slocum heard the sound of yelling voices coming closer. Maybe it had taken this long for the townspeople to work up enough courage to come see what was wrong in the jail.

Slocum stepped into the office and looked around. He spotted his Colt Navy, still in its holster with the shell belt coiled around it, lying on Sheriff Farnsworth's desk. Delaney's Smith & Wesson was there too. Both men snatched up the guns and strapped them on.

"Is there a back door?" Delaney asked anxiously.

Slocum was already looking around for a place to bolt. There didn't appear to be one. "Only way out is through the front," he said grimly. "And the sooner the better."

He hurried to the door and threw it open. The noise of the crowd was nearer now, and fresh yells went up from the townspeople as Slocum and Delaney emerged from the jail. The citizens had gathered at the edge of the square. A voice belonging to either Jed or Alvin—Slocum couldn't remember which—shouted, "It's those damn kidnappers! They killed the sheriff and they're getting away!"

The fella was jumping to a big conclusion, thought Slocum, but he was partially right: The sheriff *was* dead. And after seeing Slocum and Delaney running out of the jail, hot on the heels of all that gunfire, there was no way the citizens of Buffalo Gap would ever believe they were innocent of Farns-

worth's killing. Now they had no choice but to make a run
for it.

There had never been a choice, not really, Slocum knew.
Whatever hands of fate controlled this game moved the pieces
willy-nilly and didn't mind upsetting the board from time to
time when things didn't go to suit them. All a man could do
was hope that the players had some sort of strategy in mind,
even when it wasn't apparent.

Slocum broke into a run, heading around the squatty stone
jail building so that it would be between him and the mob. He
heard Delaney pounding along behind him. Guns started to
bang, but Slocum didn't hear any bullets coming close. In the
shadows of night like this, it took a good shot to hit anything,
and those townies weren't much as marksmen. Slocum had
that much to be thankful for.

He wondered where their horses were. There wasn't time
to find them. Any mounts would do now. He and Delaney
were already going to be running from a murder charge, so
stealing a couple of horses didn't sound so bad. Slocum angled
toward a hitch rack where several mounts were tied.

He jerked loose the reins of the first animal he came to and
vaulted into the saddle. Delaney followed suit. Only when Slocum hauled on the reins and brought his mount's head around
did he see the long ears and realize he was riding a mule
instead of a horse. Under the circumstances, he wasn't going
to complain, not as long as the mule could run. He jabbed the
heels of his boots into the animal's flanks and gripped the reins
tightly.

The mule could run, all right. It threw itself forward into a
gallop so abruptly that Slocum was almost unseated. He settled
himself in the saddle as the mule stretched out its long legs.
In a matter of moments, he had swept out of the settlement
and left the lights of Buffalo Gap behind him.

The mule not only had an opening burst like a good cow
pony, it could also maintain a high rate of speed. Slocum
glanced over his shoulder and saw that he was leaving Delaney
behind. Delaney had gotten clear of the town and seemed to

be unhurt. Slocum slowed the mule and called to Delaney, "You hit?"

"No! The shots all missed me! What now?"

"Ride like a son of a bitch!" Slocum told him. "We'll worry about where we're going later."

Luck was with them, Slocum discovered later when they slowed their headlong flight long enough for him to study the stars in the black arch of sky overhead. They had fled Buffalo Gap in a southeasterly direction, which was the way they had wanted to go in the first place. If they kept going, sooner or later they would come to Cross Plains.

"Kelso's going to beat us there," Delaney said worriedly while they were walking their mounts to rest the animals.

"Not by much," replied Slocum. "He didn't have a very big head start. And even if he makes it to Cross Plains first, that's no guarantee he'll find Rose before we do. She may not even be there."

"She's there," Delaney said softly. "I can feel it in my bones. This is almost over, John."

Slocum didn't know whether to hope his companion was right or not. He didn't want Kelso to hurt Rose, and that was a possibility if Kelso discovered he had been chasing the wrong baby. But Slocum was ready for this long chase to be over too.

There had been no signs of pursuit from Buffalo Gap. Likely the townspeople had taken a long, hard look at the bloody body of Sheriff Farnsworth and decided that they didn't want to go chasing off into the night after anybody who would cut down a lawman so mercilessly. The fact that they were wrong to blame Slocum and Delaney for the killing wouldn't enter into their thinking. They would probably send word to the Texas Rangers about the murder and jailbreak and feel that they had done their duty. Right now, thought Slocum, most of the members of that short-lived mob were probably snug in their beds, sleeping soundly.

And he would have another unjust murder charge hanging

over his head. Well, he thought philosophically, it wouldn't be the first one.

They pushed their mounts as hard as they dared. The mule Slocum was riding probably could have run all night, but the horse Delaney had grabbed didn't have that much sand. But even stopping to rest occasionally, they covered a lot of ground, and by the time the sun came up the next morning, Slocum estimated they had covered about half the distance to Cross Plains.

"We don't have any supplies now," Delaney complained as the sun rose red in the east. "And only the ammunition is in our guns. How can we get by on that?"

Slocum had a gold double eagle stashed in his right boot for emergencies. He tried to forget it was there so that he wouldn't count on it except in dire emergencies. This was shaping up to be one of those situations. The money would be enough to buy some more supplies and cartridges in Cross Plains. He might even be able to scare up a poker game and increase their stake even more, as long as they reached the settlement before word of the violence in Buffalo Gap got there. Once that news spread, he and Delaney might have to run again—and if that was the case, what would they do with Rose and Edgar, assuming the woman and the baby were even there? Maybe it would be better, thought Slocum, if Rose hadn't stayed in Cross Plains after all. It might not be a bad thing if it took them a while to locate her. That would give the furor over Farnsworth's murder time to die down a little.

But there was no point in worrying overmuch about it, he told himself. They would find what they found in Cross Plains, and deal with it as best they could. "We'll make do," he told Delaney, and left it at that.

They came to a shallow, slow-moving stream that ran in the same direction they were going and followed it. Around midday, they found themselves at a ford where a well-traveled road crossed the stream. Remembering what the rancher called Chet had said about Cross Plains, Slocum speculated that this was the stagecoach road leading to the settlement.

"I don't want to ride out here in plain sight," he said with a nod toward the road. "But we can stay parallel with this trail, and it ought to take us to Cross Plains."

"Will we be there before dark?" Delaney asked.

"Probably, but we might want to wait until after the sun's gone down to slip into town."

Delaney got a stubborn expression on his face. "I don't know if I want to wait," he said. "Kelso might find Rose before we get there."

Delaney had a point, Slocum thought. But he said noncommittally, "We'll see."

They stayed about a hundred yards south of the stage road, keeping to the trees as much as possible. This was a country of post oaks and sand roughs, and even though most of the trees had already lost their leaves, the growth was thick enough to provide cover for the riders. Slocum saw a wagon and a few horsebackers on the road during the afternoon, but none of the travelers paid any attention to him and Delaney, as far as he could tell.

By late afternoon, he had spotted two good-sized hills looming up from the plains in the distance. The hills sat closely together, with a narrow gap in between. The gap looked too narrow for the road to pass comfortably between the hills, so Slocum wasn't surprised when it swung south for several hundred yards to skirt them.

Delaney had noticed the hills too. "Those peaks look like a woman's breasts," he commented

Slocum nodded. "I suppose a fella could be put in mind of that, all right . . . if he hadn't been around a woman in a while."

Delaney rubbed the back of his hand across his mouth and said in a husky voice, "It's been a long time since I've seen Rose."

Slocum didn't say anything. He couldn't very well point out that he had made love to Delaney's wife since Delaney had. Evidently Rose hadn't minded using her body to get whatever she and Edgar needed to continue their flight from the Panhandle. Jed and Alvin had admitted they had lied about taking her in return for milk for the baby, but Rose had probably flirted with them to get what she wanted. Slocum couldn't say one way or the other what had gone on between Rose and those buffalo hunters at Snyder. He had seen the way she took care of Edgar, though. It was likely she would do whatever she had to in order to protect the child. Slocum didn't see anything dishonorable about that, but Delaney might look at it differently.

They skirted the twin hills, still giving the stage road a wide berth, and within minutes, the roofs of the buildings in Cross Plains, along with a church steeple, came into view among the trees that lined the banks of a creek. Slocum reined the mule to a halt.

"That's it, isn't it?" asked Delaney as he brought his horse to a stop alongside Slocum. "That's Cross Plains."

"I reckon it is," Slocum said.

"That's where Rose is."

Slocum didn't like the tense, strained tone of Delaney's voice. "We don't know that—" he began.

"I'm going in," Delaney said, and he heeled his horse into a run.

"Damn it!" Slocum bit out in surprise. "Delaney, you fool—"

But Delaney wasn't paying any attention to him, and Slocum knew it. Delaney was already galloping hard toward the stage road that would take him into the sleepy little frontier settlement, and there was nothing Slocum could do now except go after him.

The mule stretched out its long legs, and Slocum soon caught up with Delaney. They had already reached the stage road, however, so they were riding in plain sight toward the settlement. Slocum reached out and grabbed the reins of Delaney's horse. "Wait a minute!" he said harshly.

"Go to hell!" called Delaney. "I won't lose out to Kelso!"

And with that, he did just about the last thing Slocum would have expected him to do.

Delaney pulled the Smith & Wesson from the holster on his hip, twisted in the saddle, and fired at Slocum.

20

Slocum's instincts saved his life, as they had so many times in the past. He jerked his head to the side as Delaney fired, and the bullet whipped harmlessly past him. The sharp crack of the shot startled the mule, however, and it gave a sudden lurching jump. Already off balance from dodging Delaney's shot, Slocum felt himself slipping from the saddle. He grabbed for the horn, but his fingers slid off it without gaining enough purchase to keep him from falling.

With an angry yell, he tumbled off the mule and landed with a bone-jarring impact in the dust of the stage road.

Slocum rolled over onto his belly and gasped for air. The fall had knocked all the breath out of his lungs. He lifted his head and looked down the road toward Cross Plains. Delaney was still galloping toward the settlement, and the mule was capering along behind Delaney's horse, kicking up its heels. Slocum muttered a curse and pushed himself to his feet. He grabbed his hat from the ground where it had fallen and jammed it back on his head. A quick check told him that his gun was still in its holster. He broke into a run, heading down the road toward the town.

He wasn't sure what he was going to do when he got there, but he had come too far, spent too long on Rose's trail, to turn away from it now.

Boots weren't made for walking, let alone running, and Slocum's feet hurt like hell before he had gone a hundred yards. He kept going, though, ignoring the blisters that were forming on his feet. This east-to-west stagecoach road turned into one of the main streets of Cross Plains and intersected the military road that ran north and south. Buildings were clustered along both roads. As Slocum watched, Delaney reached the junction and swung his horse to the left, disappearing around the corner of a building.

Almost immediately, gunshots began to ring out.

What the hell! Had Kelso set a trap, been waiting to bushwhack Delaney? That was crazy, Slocum thought. When Kelso had ridden away from Buffalo Gap, Slocum and Delaney had still been locked up tight in that jail cell. Kelso might have worried that they would escape after he had fled, but surely that concern wouldn't have led him to prepare a trap. Not even a killer such as Kelso would be that suspicious of possible trouble.

But there was a chance that Delaney's unexpected arrival in Cross Plains had caught Kelso on the street, and the two men had exchanged shots. What about Rose? Was she here? Had Kelso already found her? And for that matter, what the hell had Delaney meant when he said he wasn't going to "lose out" to Kelso? Lose out on what?

The only way to answer those questions, Slocum knew, was to keep running toward the settlement.

Gunfire continued, counterpointed by angry yells and frightened screams, as Slocum reached the edge of town. He veered to the left before he got to the intersection of the two roads. He darted into an alley between a livery stable and a blacksmith's shop. As he did so, a man came out of the stable and called, "Hey, what—"

That was all Slocum had time to hear. He ran down the narrow alley and emerged behind the buildings that bordered the west side of the military road. A gap between two of them seemed to beckon him, and he dashed through it, dropping into a crouch behind a rain barrel where the alley opened onto the road. He scanned the empty street. His eyes and his nose told him there was a haze of dust in the air, an indication that mere moments earlier there had been riders and pedestrians going about their business on this road. But once the shooting had started, the street had cleared like magic as people sought cover.

One of them, in fact, had bellied down behind a water trough and was lying less than a dozen feet from Slocum. Slocum's lips drew back from his teeth in a grimace as he recognized Calvin Delaney.

Delaney had the Smith & Wesson in his hand. As Slocum watched, Delaney raised himself slightly and stuck the pistol over the top of the water trough. He fired twice toward a building across the street before ducking back down. Return fire came from the building, the bullets plunking harmlessly into the thick, pitch-coated boards of the trough. The shots originated behind a broken window in the building, which was a hardware store. Slocum caught a glimpse of Kelso as the detective fired at Delaney, then ducked back out of the window.

It was easy enough to figure out what had happened here, Slocum thought. Kelso had been on the street when Delaney had rounded the corner on horseback. The men had spotted each other, grabbed their guns, taken cover, and started trying to ventilate each other. But where was Rose?

That question was answered a second later when someone jerked open the door of the hardware store. Rose started out onto the boardwalk in front of the store, clutching Edgar tightly to her. Slocum's muscles tensed at the sight of her, blond curls flying out behind her, face twisted with fear. He started to straighten and call out to her.

But before she could clear the doorway, Kelso's arm shot out behind her and his fingers closed around the collar of her dress. He yanked her backward, the dress tearing in his brutal grip. Rose cried out as she stumbled and fell, but she managed to hang on to Edgar. Both of them fell back into the store, out of sight, and the door was kicked shut behind them.

Kelso must have had Rose and Edgar with him when Delaney came thundering into town, Slocum decided. But why? Surely Kelso had discovered by now that Edgar wasn't the baby whose kidnapping had brought him to Texas.

Such questions no longer mattered, Slocum told himself. What counted at the moment was the fact that Rose and Edgar were in mortal danger as long as they were trapped in the battle between Kelso and Delaney. Slocum was going to have to take a hand in this fight.

"Delaney!" Slocum called to the man behind the trough. Delaney looked around, his eyes wild with desperation and his gun lifting. For a second, Slocum thought Delaney was going to roll over and take another shot at him. Slocum wasn't going to let that happen again. He would shoot Delaney himself if he had to, although he would try not to kill the man.

Then Delaney got control of his raging emotions and lowered his gun. He hissed, "What do you want?"

Slocum gestured across the street. "Keep Kelso busy while I get over there."

After a second, Delaney nodded, understanding what Slocum was going to try to do. Slocum crouched lower, gathering himself for the dash across the street. He slipped the Colt Navy from the cross-draw rig and gripped it tightly in his right hand. A moment later, when Delaney opened fire on the hardware store again, Slocum darted out from behind the rain barrel and sprinted across the street at an angle that would take him to the corner of the building that was his destination.

He didn't know if Kelso fired at him or not. If the killer did, none of the shots came close enough for Slocum to hear them. Behind him, Delaney's gun fell silent, and Slocum knew the pilgrim was out of shells. It was up to him now.

Slocum reached the building and flattened his back against the wall, the Colt held ready to fire. Before he could move again, Kelso's voice rang out from inside the store. "Slocum! Delaney!" Kelso shouted. "Back off or I'll kill the woman!"

Slocum had been expecting that threat, but Delaney's reaction to it came as a surprise to him. Delaney raised his head enough to be able to shout clearly across the street, "Go ahead! The bitch doesn't mean anything to me!"

Slocum frowned. Maybe Delaney was just trying to throw Kelso off, but the sentiment had sounded genuine to Slocum. It must have to Rose too, because she let out an angry scream and shouted, "Damn you, Calvin! Damn you to hell!"

That didn't sound much like a loving wife to Slocum. He had suspected all along that Rose might have been running away from Delaney, and what was happening now tended to confirm that. The trouble between husband and wife could be dealt with later, though, after Kelso was no longer a threat.

The hardware store probably had a back door. Slocum slipped along the wall of the building toward the rear. Kelso had undoubtedly ducked into the store because it represented the nearest cover when Delaney started shooting at him; he hadn't had the luxury of picking a place that would be easy to defend. But Kelso had to be aware of that weakness, so Slocum couldn't count on having the element of surprise on his side.

He reached the rear corner and darted around to the back of the building. There was a door there, just as he had expected, along with quite a bit of litter and some empty crates. Slocum grasped the knob with his left hand, twisted it slowly. It turned. He put his shoulder against the door to hold it steady as he started to ease it open.

The door wouldn't budge. Slocum knew it wasn't locked, which meant there was probably a bar across it inside. He grimaced. If the knob had been locked, he might have been able to break the door down. With it barred or blocked in some other fashion, that was pretty unlikely. There were no windows back here, no other way into the place.

Slocum looked up at the roof. Maybe there would be some way he could get into the building up there. He holstered his gun, dragged one of the crates over beside the wall, and climbed up onto the precarious perch. He bent his knees slightly, then jumped up and grabbed the edge of the roof.

As a kid in Georgia, he had shinnied up trees like any other youngster, but since then he hadn't had much reason to do any climbing. With a grunt of effort, he hauled himself upward, threw a leg over the edge of the roof, and awkwardly scrambled up onto it. He started toward the front of the building, moving as quietly as possible. He didn't want Kelso to hear him and start throwing bullets up through the ceiling. The thought of a slug punching through the roof and ripping into his groin made him go cold all over.

Kelso had other things on his mind at the moment, Slocum saw a moment later when he reached the hardware store's false front. Peering through the window built into the false front, he saw Kelso advancing slowly into the street. Kelso had his left arm around Rose's neck, holding her tightly to him. The barrel of his gun was pressed against her temple. Rose was still holding Edgar. Slocum could see the top of the boy's head from where he was.

Delaney was standing behind the horse trough now, his gun held loosely in his hand, hanging at his side. Kelso called to him in sneering tones, "You want the woman dead, Delaney, then you go right ahead and shoot her. Maybe you'll get lucky and the bullet will go on through her and get me. But maybe you won't."

"You're taking a mighty big chance with the kid," Delaney pointed out.

"Life's a big chance," Kelso said. "All my bets have paid off so far. I think this one will too." He lifted his voice, and without turning his head called, "Slocum! I know you're around here somewhere! Don't try anything, you son of a bitch! You can't kill me quick enough to stop me from putting a bullet in this woman's brain!"

Slocum was afraid Kelso was right. The slightest pressure on the hair-trigger of the killer's revolver would mean instant death for Rose. Like it or not, all Slocum could do for the moment was wait.

"You boys just don't give up, do you?" said Kelso. "You've chased this woman and the kid halfway across

Texas—but I got to 'em first. Now the payoff's going to be mine.''

Payoff? What payoff? Kelso was working for the Mulwrays, looking for their kidnapped nephew Kenneth. Edgar Delaney wasn't worth anything . . . except to the people who loved him.

"You don't have to do this," Rose said suddenly to Kelso. "I'll come with you willingly, mister. I'd rather give the boy up than see any harm come to him."

"Too late for that," Kelso said heavily. "Your husband there isn't going to let us go without a fight."

"Damn right I'm not," Delaney said. "I've worked too hard to get that kid." He started to lift his gun.

Slocum wasn't sure what sort of bluff Delaney intended to pull with that empty Smith & Wesson, but he didn't care. Delaney was about to prod Kelso into killing Rose, and Slocum didn't want that. Nor could he risk a shot at Kelso while Rose and Edgar were so close to him. The .36-caliber slugs in the Colt Navy were heavy enough so that they might pass through Kelso's body and hit the woman or the child. No, he had to distract Kelso somehow, give Rose a chance to get away from him.

One of the boards that angled from the back of the false front to the roof was right beside Slocum. He bent, hooked his hands under the board, and hauled upward with all his strength. With a squeal of nails, the support pulled out of the roof.

And the false front began to sag forward.

"What the hell!" Kelso exclaimed. He twisted halfway around. Slocum slammed his shoulder into the false front, making it lean even more. There were support boards at the corners, holding it in place, but they were weakening under the weight of the structure. Slocum hit it again with his shoulder, and more nails screeched as they pulled free of the wood. The false front toppled, dropping Slocum with it.

Slocum had been counting on Kelso being so startled by the sight of the false front falling toward him that he wouldn't pull the trigger and shoot Rose. That was what happened. Rose jerked out of Kelso's grasp and threw herself to one side, away from the falling boards, taking Edgar with her. Kelso went the other way. The false front, carrying Slocum with it, crashed to the street, shearing off the porch roof over the front of the hardware store in the process and raising a huge cloud of dust. Slocum landed with stunning force. He wasn't sure where Kelso was. He hoped the false front had landed on the gunman when it fell. That would have put Kelso out of action.

Instead, a gun roared somewhere close by and a bullet kicked up splinters from the debris of the shattered false front. Slocum rolled, bringing up the gun he had managed to hang on to during the jarring fall from the roof. Pain shot through him, and he didn't know if one of Kelso's bullets had found him or if he had broken his ribs. Either way, he fought through the red waves of pain that tried to engulf him and came up in a crouch, his eyes watering from the thick clouds of dust billowing in the air as he searched for Kelso.

He didn't have to look for very long. Kelso charged, the long duster flapping behind him, six-gun in one hand and the sawed-off shotgun in the other. The hammer of Kelso's pistol clicked on an empty chamber in the cylinder. He started to bring up the scattergun.

Slocum squeezed off two shots, triggering so quickly and smoothly that the pair of reports blended into one roar of exploding powder. The bullets thudded into Kelso's chest and drove him backward. Both barrels of the shotgun went off as Kelso jerked the triggers involuntarily in his dying convulsion, but the weapon was pointed almost straight up by the time it discharged. The buckshot went harmlessly into the air, then peppered back down into the street like a brief shower of lead sleet. One of the pellets bounced off Slocum's shoulder, but he barely noticed it.

He kicked aside the rubble of the fallen false front and walked over to Kelso. The gunman lay on his back, the front of his shirt drenched in blood. He stared up at Slocum with rapidly glazing eyes, and his mouth opened. No sound came out. His mouth stayed open, and so did his eyes. The light in them died. No longer did they remind Slocum of a snake's eyes. Now they might as well have been chunks of glass.

Slocum swung around, looking for Rose. He thought she had gotten clear of the falling false front. The dust was beginning to settle now. He spotted her a few yards away, leaning against a hitch rack in front of the building next to the hardware store. She seemed to be all right, and so did Edgar. Judging by the sound of the frightened crying coming from the boy, there was nothing wrong with his lungs. He was wailing loudly.

Up and down the street, heads began to pop out of buildings. Now that the trouble was over, people would emerge from their hiding places to find out what in the world had happened. It must have seemed to them that a war had broken out in their peaceful little settlement.

Delaney still stood across the street, looking stunned by everything that had happened. As Slocum started toward Rose, though, so did Delaney. Slocum saw him coming from the corner of his eye.

Rose turned her head as she tried to comfort the terrified Edgar, and when she saw Delaney, she screamed at Slocum, "Look out! He'll kill us all!"

Slocum's eyes widened in surprise. He started to tell Rose that Delaney was out of bullets, but then he saw Delaney's gun coming up. Delaney's thumb looped over the hammer of the Smith & Wesson and started to pull it back—

Slocum did what his instincts were screaming at him to do. He pivoted sharply and fired from the hip, letting nerves and muscles with years of experience guide the shot. The slug took Delaney in the belly and doubled him over so that when Delaney's gun went off, the bullet smacked into the ground in front of him. He staggered, tried to lift the gun again, and Slocum shot him a second time. This time the bullet flung him backward. Delaney landed in the street and lay motionless, in the same sort of graceless sprawl of death as Kelso. Slocum strode over to him, keeping the Colt trained on him just in case, and kicked the gun away from his hand. When Slocum was satisfied that Delaney was dead, he holstered his own gun and picked up the Smith & Wesson, wincing in pain as he bent over to retrieve the weapon. He broke it open and checked the cylinder.

It was full.

Delaney had been holding out, Slocum thought with a grim smile as he snapped the revolver closed. Concealed somewhere on him, Delaney had had more cartridges for the Smith & Wesson. If not for Rose's warning, he could have walked right up to them and gunned down both of them.

But why? Had that been Delaney's plan all along, to murder Rose, and Slocum too, when they caught up to the woman and the boy?

He faced Rose, ignoring the pain in his side that made him want to sit down somewhere and rest for about a week. It was time for some answers, and he intended to get them. But first there was something else he had to know.

"Are you all right?" he asked. "Is Edgar hurt?"

Rose looked up at him, her blue eyes as compelling as ever. "I'm fine," she said in the husky voice he remembered so well, "and so is the boy. But his name's not Edgar."

Slocum stiffened. All the little things that had been bothering him for days now suddenly shifted around in his mind and locked together, forming a pattern that finally made a picture. He stood there silently, too stunned for a moment to say anything.

"His name is Kenneth," Rose went on. "Kenneth Mulwray."

21

The Camino Real was the fanciest hotel in El Paso. Slocum wasn't surprised that Steven and Sheila Mulwray were staying there. Nothing but the best would do for some folks.

As for himself and Rose, he was sure they looked somewhat out of place as they walked across the ornately decorated lobby toward the hotel dining room. The ride from Cross Plains had been long, hard, and dusty, and they hadn't taken the time to change clothes or clean up after the trip. Rose wanted to get this over with as quickly as possible, and so did Slocum.

The clerk behind the desk started to come out and stop them, but he came to a sudden halt when he saw the look Slocum turned toward him. Slocum's face was lean, hard, and grizzled from the trip. He was in no mood for any nonsense. He and Rose walked past the clerk. Slocum figured the man might send for the law, and that was another reason for him and Rose to take care of their business quickly. There was still a little matter of a murder charge, unjustified though it might be, in the case of Sheriff Farnsworth from Buffalo Gap.

Slocum and Rose stepped through the arched doorway into the hotel dining room. It took only a second for Slocum's keen eyes to spot the Mulwrays. They were sitting at a table in the corner, flanked by a couple of potted plants. The table was

177

covered with a fine linen cloth and set with the finest silver and crystal. There was a bottle of wine on the table, and Sheila Mulwray was sipping from the glass she held in her hand when she noticed Slocum and Rose coming toward the table. Her green eyes widened in shock, and the wine glass slipped from her hand, spilling its dark red contents across the sparkling white tablecloth. Slocum thought the wine looked like blood.

"Good Lord!" Steven Mulwray exclaimed as Sheila spilled the wine. He saw her stunned expression, which was directed over his shoulder, and as he started to turn around, he said, "What's wrong—"

Slocum came to a stop beside Mulwray's chair and gave the man a curt nod. "Mr. Mulwray," he said. Then he glanced at Sheila and added in a voice as cold as that blue norther that had blown down from the plains several weeks earlier, "Ma'am."

Mulwray stood up. He said, "I didn't expect to see you again, Mr. Slocum." He looked at Rose. "Is this the lady you and your friend were looking for?"

"That's right," Slocum said.

Mulwray gave Rose a polite smile. "I'm pleased to meet you, Mrs. . . . Delaney, was it?"

"I wasn't his wife," Rose said flatly. "We lived together, and I took his name, but we never stood up in front of a preacher."

"Oh. I see." It was clear from Mulwray's puzzled expression that he didn't, though. He glanced at his own wife, saw that her face was still pale and drawn, and frowned as he said, "Sheila, what in the world is the matter?"

"Your wife didn't expect to see us again either," said Slocum. "She figured Delaney would kill Rose and me as soon as he got the chance, and Kenneth too."

Mulwray's frown deepened. "Kenneth?" he repeated. "What do you know about my nephew? What's going on here? I demand some answers, Mr. Slocum!"

Slocum looked at Sheila. "Your husband wants answers. Should I give them to him, or will you?"

"I don't know what you're talking about," Sheila said coldly. "Steven, this man has lost his mind. I think you should summon some assistance and have him removed from the hotel."

"You don't want to do that," Slocum told Mulwray. "Not if you ever want to see that boy again."

Mulwray's voice hardened. "You have Kenneth? What do you want, money? It's true there's a reward—"

"That's what Kelso was after," Slocum declared. "All he wanted was the money you'd offered for the safe return of the boy." He nodded toward Sheila. "Your wife and Delaney wanted more. They wanted everything. And they figured out how to get it."

Sheila Mulwray pushed back her chair. "I'm not going to sit here and listen to this nonsense—"

"Wait a minute, Sheila," her husband said sharply. "I want to hear what Mr. Slocum has to say."

Sheila hesitated, then bit her lip and settled back down in the chair. Her hands dropped into her lap.

Slocum put a hand on Rose's arm. She would have to start this story off, but she would need strength to get through it. He squeezed her arm to let her know that he would be right there beside her.

"Calvin and I kidnapped your nephew, Mr. Mulwray," she began, her voice shaky and tentative. "I . . . I'm sorry we did it. Calvin said that you were rich, that you'd never miss the money you'd pay us as ransom. But he promised me the boy wouldn't be hurt. As soon as we got the money, we'd send him back to you."

Mulwray looked solemnly at her. "That's a shocking confession, young woman. I'll have to send for the authorities."

"Hold off on that," advised Slocum, "until you've heard the rest of it."

"I was disguised as a man," Rose said, resuming her story. "We got into your house. Calvin . . . had a key."

That brought another frown from Mulwray.

"We took the baby and ran. Calvin said we would take him

to El Paso, and you would send the ransom money there.''
Rose looked at Slocum. "We really were headed for Santa Fe
when I met you, John. But from there, we planned to go on
down to El Paso. We just weren't expecting such a bad storm
as the one that hit up in the Panhandle. I should have known,
since I was born in Texas, but I didn't live here long. My
folks moved to Illinois when I was just a baby.''

"I don't understand any of this," snapped Mulwray. "If
you're telling the truth about the kidnapping, why did you take
Kenneth and leave your husband?''

Rose looked him straight in the eye. "Because I found out
that he was planning to kill Kenneth after we got the ransom
money. I couldn't let him do that.''

"The son of a bitch," breathed Mulwray. "Why would he
kill an innocent child?''

Slocum said, "Because that was his deal with your wife.''

"That's a terrible lie!" Sheila burst out. "How can you say
such things?''

Rose reached into her dress and brought out a folded piece
of paper. "Because I have this," she said. "The letter you
wrote to Calvin with the rest of his instructions. He picked it
up when we stopped in Wichita, just like the two of you
planned. You'd told him to burn it after he read it, but he
didn't. He was going to keep it and use it to blackmail you if
he didn't get his share of the money. I found it, and that's
how I knew he was going to murder Kenneth.''

Sheila started up from her chair, her hand darting out toward
the paper. "Give me that, you slut!''

Rose jerked the letter back, out of Sheila's reach. "Not
hardly. It's going to the law." She glared at Sheila. "And you
ought to be careful who you're calling a slut, ma'am, after
what Calvin told me about the things you and he did behind
your husband's back. I guess that was the way you got him
to go along with whatever you wanted.''

Slowly, his face like stone, Steven Mulwray turned toward
his wife. "Sheila, is any of this true?''

"Of course not! They're mad! They're making it all up. I

wouldn't betray you, Steven, and I'd never have anything to do with hurting Kenneth!''

Slocum took the letter from Rose. "This says otherwise.'' He held it out to Mulwray. "You can read it yourself if you want, but I'm not handing it over to anybody except the law.''

Mulwray glanced at the writing on the paper, and his skin turned gray as he scanned the words. Haggard lines appeared on his face. "That's my wife's handwriting,'' he said.

Slocum took up the story. He knew the rest of it well enough to tell it. "Rose and Delaney dyed the baby's hair a darker color and pretended he was theirs. Then, while they were making their way across the Panhandle, Rose found out Delaney was planning to kill the boy. She took him and slipped off from Delaney after they argued, then ran into me. Right then, after what had happened with Delaney, she didn't trust anybody, so she kept running, planning to get back down to a town called Cross Plains, where she had relatives from when she was a kid herself. Delaney found me in Tascosa and heard that I was looking for a woman and a baby, and he knew they had to be Rose and your nephew. Same thing happened with Kelso. We were all after the same kid, only I thought he was Edgar Delaney, not Kenneth Mulwray. I was the only one who was fooled, though.''

"No,'' said Mulwray. "I was deceived too.''

Slocum thought about how Delaney and Sheila had acted when they met at Charley Goodnight's ranch. "I reckon so,'' Slocum said. "They played us for fools, Mulwray, and they damned near got away with it.''

Mulwray took a deep breath. He wouldn't look at his wife now, pointedly keeping his eyes turned away from her. "What happened?'' he asked. "Where are Delaney and Kelso now?''

"Both dead. Kelso caught up to Rose first, in that settlement I mentioned called Cross Plains. Delaney and I got there a little later. There was some gunplay, and the truth came out. It was nearly too late . . . but not quite.''

Mulwray passed a hand over his weary face. "This is an

incredible story. Why . . . why would anyone do such a thing?''

''So that your wife could have everything,'' Rose said. ''Calvin told me all about it, after I confronted him with that letter. He bragged about how he helped your wife sabotage your brother's boat so that it would sink. They were all supposed to drown in the lake, but Kenneth wasn't in the boat. So your wife had to come up with some other way to get rid of him, and she thought of setting up a phony kidnapping. The ransom was going to be Calvin's payoff, but he had to kill the baby so that your brother's share of the shipping company would come to you, Mr. Mulwray.''

''Then, when a little more time had passed, she would have found a way to get rid of you too, Mulwray,'' Slocum said. ''The whole thing probably would have worked . . . if Rose hadn't taken off with the baby.''

Mulwray looked at Rose. ''Then, I . . . I suppose I owe you my life, young lady. Thank you. Where . . . where is Kenneth now?''

''In a safe place,'' said Slocum. ''We didn't want to bring him with us to the hotel until we were sure you believed us about everything.''

Mulwray turned his head and finally looked at Sheila again. She returned his gaze with a cool, defiant stare. He looked back at Slocum. ''I believe you,'' he said simply. ''I thought I knew my wife, but it's clear now that I don't.''

''We'll see that the child is returned to you,'' Rose said, and it was obvious from the strain in her voice that she didn't want to be parted from Kenneth. She was willing to do whatever was best for the boy, though, Slocum knew.

''You're going to need somebody to help you take care of the kid,'' Slocum said to Mulwray, a faint grin on his face. ''Maybe something could be worked out with a judge so that Rose could give you a hand.''

Slocum saw the sudden light of hope in Rose's eyes and the way that Mulwray seemed to be considering the suggestion.

He also saw the derringer in Sheila's hand as she lifted it from her lap.

"No!" Sheila cried in a ragged voice. "You've ruined everything, but I won't let you take my place, damn you!"

Slocum's left arm shot out and swept Rose aside as the derringer cracked. The bullet whipped harmlessly through the space where Rose had been an instant earlier. The confrontation had drawn the attention of everyone else in the dining room, and people screamed and went diving for cover at the sound of the shot. The derringer had two barrels, but before Sheila could fire the second one, Slocum lunged toward her and drove his loosely bunched fist across her jaw. Her head jerked to the side and she sagged back against her chair. Slocum plucked the derringer from her hand.

"You'd better hang on to that," he said to Mulwray as he put the little pistol in the man's hand. Mulwray was clearly shaken by everything he had seen and heard in the last few minutes. "And don't turn your back on her too often while you're trying to get everything hashed out with the law."

Mulwray nodded. "I . . . I won't."

Slocum turned to Rose and put his hands on her shoulders. He bent and quickly kissed her. "I've got to be riding," he said. "The town marshal's probably on his way already. Take good care of yourself . . . and the boy."

"I will," she promised softly. "Good-bye, John. And—thank you. Thank you so much for coming after me."

"Had to," Slocum said with another grin. "You stole my horse."

He was riding that rangy lineback dun when he left El Paso a few minutes later, heading east along the road that followed the Rio Grande. A long time ago—or at least what seemed like a long time ago—he had been bound for San Antonio, planning to spend the winter there. That still sounded like a good idea to him.

Rose and Mulwray could handle everything that needed to be done from here on out. Rose and Slocum had left Kenneth with a kindly widow woman at a boardinghouse on the edge of town. Soon Kenneth would be back with his uncle, if that reunion hadn't taken place already. And as for Rose, well, Slocum didn't know what would happen to her, but at least she would have a chance for a better life if the authorities cooperated. With Mulwray on her side, Slocum had a feeling that would come about.

Come spring, mused Slocum, he might head back up to the Panhandle and see if Lady Arabella Winthrop was still running the Deuces in Tascosa. Maybe Bat Masterson and Billy Dixon would come back for another season of buffalo hunting, and he could join up with them for a while. If not, Charley Goodnight would need extra men for the spring roundup, and Slocum could make a pretty fair hand when he put his mind to it. . . .

He was so busy thinking about the future that he almost didn't see the past come charging out of a brush thicket alongside the Rio Grande, guns blazing. Slocum jerked to the side as a bullet sang past his head, and the sudden movement made a twinge of pain shoot out from his ribs, which hadn't been broken after all but had been bruised pretty good by the fall back in Cross Plains. Those injuries would never get a chance to heal completely if Slocum didn't move fast now.

He tried to pull the dun aside as Mace Jones galloped out of the brush on a big steeldust. Slocum's reaction wasn't quite fast enough, and the horses crashed together and went down in a welter of flailing legs. Slocum kicked his feet free of the stirrups as the dun fell. He slammed into the trail and rolled quickly to the side, trying to get out of reach of the lashing hooves. As Slocum came up on his knees, he saw Mace scrambling to his feet a few yards away.

"Now I've got you, you bastard!" Mace howled. He had dropped the revolver he had been firing at Slocum a moment earlier, before the collision, but his big hand swooped down to his belt and plucked out the heavy-bladed Bowie knife. He lunged at Slocum, shouting, "I'll skin you alive!"

Slocum palmed out the Colt as he lurched to his feet. He

fired, the bullet thudding into Mace's chest. The impact of the shot made the vengeance-crazed buffalo hunter stumble, but he kept coming. Slocum pulled the trigger again and again, emptying the Colt. Puffs of dust came from Mace's coat as each of the slugs crashed into his body. He staggered on, the Bowie upraised. Slocum tensed, ready to throw himself aside. What the hell was it going to take to put Mace down?

Then the buffalo hunter tripped and pitched forward, landing facedown in the dirt at Slocum's feet. The knife fell from his hand. A shudder went through the great hulk, and Slocum heard the death rattle in Mace's throat.

Slocum's side was hurting like blazes again. He ignored the pain as he reloaded his pistol, then walked down the river road to catch his horse, which had scrambled up and trotted off skittishly. He didn't look back at Mace. Instead, he swung up into the saddle with a grimace and heeled the dun into a fast gait that carried him eastward away from the dead man.

That was what he got for thinking about the future, Slocum told himself. The here and now was enough for him. He rode on, hoping it would be a while before somebody tried to kill him again.